THREE TRAILS
TO TRIANGLE

THREE TRAILS
TO TRIANGLE

A WESTERN STORY

ROBERT J. HORTON

BLACKSTONE
PUBLISHING

Printed in the United States of America

ISBN 978-1-5384-7474-7
Fiction / Westerns

1 3 5 7 9 10 8 6 4 2

CIP data for this book is available
from the Library of Congress

Blackstone Publishing
31 Mistletoe Rd.
Ashland, OR 97520

www.BlackstonePublishing.com

CHAPTER ONE

A bright, shining mark—the new State Bank of Milton.

It stood on the southwest corner of Main and Center Streets, the two short, principal thoroughfares of the old cow town, and its red bricks furnished a dazzling contrast to the weather-beaten buildings clustered about it under the spreading branches of the cottonwoods in that oasis in the broad, burning plain. The July sun struck the gold from the lettering of the sign on its plate glass windows and brought out the crimson of its outer walls.

This was the dull season and the town seemed to sleep in the shade of its trees. A stranger would wonder at the pretentious little bank, little suspecting the treasure it held; wondering, perhaps, if it did sufficient business to warrant such housing. But Milton was the supply point for the northwest portion of the north range. It was prosperous despite its drab appearance, and the bank served a vast territory in which were many large ranches. It was sound and respected, and its board of directors included a dozen important and influential stockmen who numbered their herds by the thousand head.

And Milton was on the railroad, which was important.

East of town a shadow shot like a ball of lead out of a cloud of swirling dust. Leaving the dust behind him as he slowed his horse, a rider cantered to the trees growing on the banks of a stream. He allowed his mount a taste of the water, forded the creek, and dismounted on the west bank. He was a small, wasp-like man, alert of movement, dark-skinned, with beetling black eyes and a long, thin nose. He took tobacco and papers from his shirt pocket and rolled a cigarette with nervous fingers, eyeing his horse the while.

"Ten miles all told at half speed," he mused in an undertone. "Two slow miles to town, then five at full speed … and the mountains when we want 'em." His teeth flashed in a smile as he snapped a match into flame and lighted his smoke.

He strode to the edge of the trees and looked toward a smudge of green two miles away on the yellow plain which was the town of Milton. A faint smile played on his lips and his hand rested lightly on the butt of his gun. It was an hour past noon.

Half an hour later he swung into the saddle. The sweat that had been streaming on his horse's neck and flanks was dry, the hair matted with dust ridges. The man jogged across the intervening space of prairie toward town, slumped in the saddle, his hat pulled far down over his eyes, his attitude that of a rider who had ridden slow and far in the hot sun. As a matter of fact, he had ridden the ten miles at "half speed" from where he had spent the night, and now was laboring into town with the hour of his arrival expertly timed. The State Bank of Milton closed business for the day at four o'clock.

Mort Seymour, the cashier, was at the front window of the cage. Sylvester Graham—only a very favored few dared call him Sil—the president, was at his new desk in the private office in the rear of the bank. A large, pompous man, with black eyebrows and a bristly gray mustache, he was the financial power of fully a quarter of the great north range. Allied with him were all the influential stockmen of the district. He was a man who commanded respect as is becoming to the head of an important institution. He was cold, hard, inexorable in his dealings, always with the best interests of the bank uppermost in his mind, guiding his judgment.

These two men, then—Seymour, the hireling, and Graham, the master—were in the bank half an hour before closing time on this hot July afternoon.

Seymour, glancing out the front window, saw a tired-looking rider pull up in front of the bank and dismount. The rider left his horse standing with reins dangling and entered the bank somewhat hesitatingly, his snapping, black eyes searching out every corner of the cage and centering on the open door of the private office before they met those of the cashier, who frowned slightly because the man was a stranger.

"This looks like a good bank," said the newcomer in a querulous voice, approaching the window. "Brand new, ain't it?"

"It is new," replied Seymour with a superior lift of his brows. He permitted himself to add: "The most modern bank north of the Falls, not excepting Bend City. You have some business to transact?"

"I've been in Bend City," the stranger volunteered. "That's the county seat. Nice town, but my business ain't out that way. I want to put some money in a bank up here and I heard about this one. That's why I'm here." He had raised his voice slightly as he said the last words and had the satisfaction of glimpsing a form in the private office as Graham looked out into the cage a moment.

"You wish to make a deposit?" Seymour said, business-like, as he reached for a deposit slip. "How much do you wish to deposit?"

It was rapidly nearing closing time and the stranger was watching the clock on the partition that separated the private office from the cage.

"Well, I wanted to deposit quite a bit," he explained with a thin smile, "and I wanted to be sure it was a good, strong bank. I ain't had much faith in banks because they get held up every now and then and I ain't got any money to lose." He was speaking in a voice that just carried into the private office.

The cashier gave him a clear, cold stare. "I trust you're not questioning the strength of *this* bank," he said severely. "The strength of this bank was thoroughly established years before this new building was erected. And the State Bank of Milton never has been held up."

"That's what I heard"—the stranger nodded eagerly—"and that's why I came here. Oh, I guess it's a strong bank, all right. I was told as much, or I wouldn't have packed my cash all the way from Bend City here."

At the word cash the cashier pricked up his ears. More often than not, new accounts were opened with a check on another bank, or with stockmen's checks on the Milton bank. He surveyed the man on the other side of the window. Usually it was a person who had a hundred dollars or so to put into a bank who was most concerned about its safeguarding his deposit. And the stranger didn't look like ready money, although his shirt and scarf and hat were of excellent quality. His manner was so simple that the cashier almost snorted in making his reply.

"There is such a thing as putting so much cash into this bank that we would have to take extra precautions," he said sarcastically.

The stranger thought he heard a chuckle in the private office. "Oh, you must have a strong safe," he said, his jaw dropping.

"My dear man," said Seymour in exasperation, "we have the newest thing in burglar-proof vaults, and the first automatic alarm brought into this country. But every penny could be taken out of our vault and the bank would still be good for your money, regardless of how much it is. We don't keep *all* our money in the vault, you know."

The stranger was staring absently past the cashier at the clock. "Well, I hope you don't think I'm finicky," he said apologetically. "Naturally, when a man's makin' a deposit of cash money in a bank he wants to know somethin' about the bank he's puttin' it in. That's natural, ain't it? You don't blame me for askin' a question or two, do you?"

"No, of course not," answered the cashier, relenting. "It's nearing closing time, and if you'll tell me your name and the amount you wish to deposit, I'll make out the slip for you."

"That's kind of you," said the prospective customer, drawing a thick wallet from inside his shirt. "I was readin' a bank advertisement in the *Great Falls Tribune* where it said something about a bank's first business bein' service, or something like that. I reckon you feel the same way about it. I can't write, so if you'll make out the papers, I'll appreciate it. But don't think that just because I can't write, I can't make money. Gettin' money is the easiest thing I do, and I'll bet you I get more than double what I put in in no time."

"No doubt," said the cashier out of the corner of his mouth. "What's the name?" he asked, his pen poised over the deposit slip.

"Crow," was the answer, almost in a moan. "Joseph Crow."

"And the address?" queried the cashier, writing down the name.

"Well, you just better make it Milton," replied Crow.

"Joseph Crow, Milton," intoned the cashier. "And how much?"

The stranger removed a wide rubber band that secured the wallet and opened it. "We'll see," he said, as if to himself. "I'm not sure how much is here. I've spent some, you know, and I'll have to count it. But it's quite a bit."

He flashed a glance at the clock as he drew a sheaf of bills from the wallet. "These are hundreds," he pointed out. "Don't mistake 'em for tens. I lost a hundred-dollar bill once, or ninety dollars of it, because a man took it for a ten and I couldn't correct him until it was too late. Yes, sir. You can see these are all hundred-dollar bills, can't you?" He ruffled them under the astonished eyes of the cashier.

"Yes, I'm accustomed to counting money. A hundred-dollar bill is nothing new to me. I wouldn't be here if I couldn't tell a hundred from a ten … and count them fast into the bargain."

"I suppose you're right. Now don't touch that stack till I get these others out of the other side." The stranger brought forth another sheaf of bills. "These are fifties and twenties, with some tens and fives … I don't know how many. I'll have to keep about a hundred dollars for cash in my pocket besides what one-dollar bills and silver I've got. I've only got a little gold on me and I'll keep that. I don't like to carry much gold because it's too heavy and wears out my pockets. I reckon you don't see many one-dollar bills, either, do you? I got these down south on the main line of the railroad where Eastern folks bring them in and leave 'em. They can't refuse to take 'em, you know … the storekeepers and such that get 'em, I mean. I don't suppose you could refuse 'em, either, could you? Maybe you've got a bunch of 'em right now." He peered up at the cashier questioningly.

"We don't refuse anything which is legal tender," said the cashier in a more respectful tone. His practiced eye showed him that there was considerable money in the banknotes under his nose. "Perhaps I can count it faster than you can, if you don't mind."

"Wait till I separate these fifties, twenties, and tens into different piles. There, you see? I've run into a one! I don't know how it got in there. I've got a bunch of them in my pocket, and I didn't know …"

"It's four o'clock, Mort," came a sharp voice from the door of the private office. "Close up and bring that man in here to count the money and make his deposit. Him standing there at the window after hours will attract attention."

"Oh, I don't want to make any bother," said the stranger quickly, clutching at the bills. "If you're goin' to close up, I'll just come in in the mornin', although I don't like to be packin' all this cash around any longer than I can help. But I want to see it counted right and everything shipshape when I put it in."

"Send him in here," Sylvester Graham ordered impatiently.

The cashier came out the rear of the cage and, after locking the front door of the bank, led the reluctant stranger into the private office of Sylvester Graham.

"Bring the deposit slip and a book," Graham ordered Seymour. Then he looked coldly at the stranger, who was standing in front of the desk with his wallet and the bills in his hands.

"I overheard you tell my cashier you wished to make a deposit," the bank president said sternly. He was not a man to waste time or words with a simpleton who was suspicious of banks, even though the man before him might make a considerable deposit.

"Yes, I heard this was a good bank …"

"Never mind what you've heard elsewhere, my man," said Graham pompously. "I'm the president of this bank and you can take my word for it that it's a good one. Nobody is going to get your money out of here, once you've put it in, except yourself. Now put your bills on the table and we'll count them and have this transaction over with. I don't usually stay after hours. Count that money, Mort, and make out the slip."

The stranger had put the bills on the desk, and now the cashier ran through them rapidly, counting them twice.

"Five thousand two hundred and eighty-five dollars," he announced, looking at Graham.

"Is that right? Do you see him count 'em?" the stranger asked Graham.

For answer the bank president took the bills and counted them himself. "That's correct," he snapped, when he had finished. "Do you wish me to count them slowly for you?"

"Oh, I guess it ain't necessary," was the answer.

"All right, Mort, put the amount on the slip," said Graham. "Let's see. Joseph Crow, eh? And you're expecting to live or do business around here? I see you've given your residence as Milton."

"I expect to do business around here," Crow said, nodding.

"All right, sign your name as you always sign it on this line. I've made a cross on the line, and then sign it again on the line below. That's so we cannot mistake your signature in case you should draw a check." He shoved the signature card across the desk and pointed to the lines.

"I'll have to make my mark," said Crow meekly.

"*Humph.*" The banker frowned. "If you can only make a cross for your name, you will have to come to the bank in person, I guess, if you should want money. Usually in such cases we ..."

"Oh, I've got a mark everybody can't make," said Crow. "I'll take a chance on anybody forging it. Anyway, I don't expect to draw any checks."

Graham brightened just a trifle and frowned quickly to conceal it. "Where did you get this money, by the way?" he asked. "We like to know something about a new customer. In fact, it's one of our ... *er* ... rules." He cleared his throat impressively.

"What difference does it make?" demanded Crow, with his first show of spirit. "Of course, if you've got to know, I got it down south."

"I see." The banker nodded. "Sold something, or ...?"

"I took it from a bank, of course," blurted Crow.

"Yes, naturally," said Graham hastily. "Withdrew it because you would need capital up here. What is your business?"

"My own," answered Crow belligerently. "Now if you want to

see my mark, I'll draw it for you and then you can see what you think of it."

"Very well," agreed the nettled banker, his curiosity getting the better of him for once, although he glanced sharply at his cashier to make sure he wasn't smiling.

The new customer took the proffered pen and bent over the signature card, shading what he drew with his hand. He straightened suddenly and handed the card to Graham. The banker looked at the crude drawing of a black bird with a sharp, pointed bill.

Then he remembered the name, Joseph Crow. He looked up with a thunderstruck expression of incredulity in his eyes. Then he got quickly to his feet.

"The Crow!" he cried.

The western sun shone through the rear window and glinted on the blue barrel of the gun that leaped into the stranger's hand as the man gave vent to a jeering laugh.

"Don't get active!" was the sharp warning. "You recognize the trademark of the Crow, but the name on paper went over your head and over your clerk's head, too." Again, that jarring laugh. "I could have come in just before closin', but I always aim to have a bit of fun out of every job. It's a nice new bank you've got, and you've never been robbed, eh? Everything I told your clerk here was true. I came here because you've got a good, strong bank, and I don't intend to draw any checks. You're sure you know me?" His expression had changed. The beetling black eyes were charged with menace, the voice was hissing but clear, the face was mean and drawn.

"I know the mark," said Graham, his own features frozen into a glare. "I don't doubt but that you're that blackguard and thief and murderer known as the Crow. But you're in the wrong territory this trip. What do you want?"

"Me?" The Crow chuckled. "I want money. Now we'll finish this transaction at once. Go out there, you, and bring in your cash." He waved Seymour toward the cage. "I'm goin' to stand right here inside the office where I can see you through the door, and if you make any slips, I'm goin' to pour hot lead in you. Give me those keys first."

The cashier turned over the keys as ordered. His face was white. Sylvester Graham laughed. In that instant the Crow whirled on him and struck him in the mouth with the heavy barrel of his gun with such force that the banker was knocked into his chair, spitting out teeth and blood.

"Next time I'll shoot," said the bandit quietly. "Do as I told you, clerk. Never mind the gold or silver and leave out the one-dollar bills."

"Sheriff Hal Drew will have you in forty-eight hours, and the stockmen will string you up with me helping," sputtered Graham in a fearful rage.

"I'll give your trick sheriff seventy-two hours to get me and then send you back a couple hundred to live on till next payday," was the outlaw's sneering answer. "Don't talk much. I don't like you and I've got an easy thumb that loves to fan a pistol hammer."

Seymour came in with a tray loaded with packages of bills.

"Bring the rest from the vault and see that they're big ones," the Crow ordered. "Do as I say, or I'll drop the two of you and help myself. Hustle, unless you're ready to check in for a harp."

Seymour brought more money, white-faced and shaking, while Graham waved a feeble hand in futile protest. The bandit stuffed the bills inside his shirt until it bulged about his waist. He crammed bills into all his pockets and filled the crown of his hat. His own money and his wallet he stuffed into his boots.

"Lock that door!" he commanded the cashier, indicating the door leading into the cage and handing the man the keys.

The cashier obeyed.

"Which key locks this door?" purred the outlaw in a deadly tone, pointing to the other door of the office that led into the corridor outside. "I'll find out quick enough if you name the wrong one, and I know the big one is to the front door because I saw you use it. You pair are sure in a bad way, but I'm lettin' you off easy at that."

Seymour held the proper key out from the ring and the Crow took the bunch. "You'll start shoutin' soon enough and that'll be all right for me," he said grimly. "I'll get half an hour's start or more and that's more than I need. I'll just stick this card with my mark on it outside the front door and maybe that'll attract attention quicker than your fuss will. Tell Sheriff Drew your bank's been robbed at last, Sil, and give him the Crow's compliments."

The bandit's laugh sounded harshly in the ears of his victims as he locked them in the office and let himself out the front door. In less than a minute he was riding up the street toward the west and, behind him, sticking in the door of the bank, was a signature card bearing the crude drawing in ink of a black bird with a sharp, pointed bill—the most feared symbol of outlawry in the north range country.

CHAPTER TWO

A weary posse trailed down through the foothills twenty miles west of Milton. Sheriff Hal Drew rode at the head of his score of men, his face fixed in a frown. He stroked his mustaches thoughtfully and there was no glimmer of defeat in his eyes—only grave reflection. The raid of the notorious outlaw who styled himself the Crow upon the State Bank of Milton was a serious matter. It set a dangerous precedent, for one thing, and the presence of the lone bandit in the country constituted a menace to law and order, and the safety of life and property, which could not be ignored. And the Crow had slipped through the fingers, so to speak, of the posse with the ease of a meadowlark flying through a barbed wire fence. The sheriff considered this a personal insult, despite the bandit's reputation for being posse-proof, and the insolent manner in which Sylvester Graham had been treated and the bank robbed of more than $20,000 had roused the stockmen. It was as mean a case as Hal Drew, sheriff of Bend County, had had on his hands during his tenure of nearly three terms of office.

And Drew was due to receive another shock before he rode

out of the hills. He had led his men—a picked company—into the high hills because those tracks he had been able to pick up led in that direction, and the mountains offered innumerable hiding places and an intricate network of side trails where fresh tracks would instantly disclose the bandit's passing on any of them. He had dispatched messengers north and south, in the event the Crow held to the prairie country and had sent out a general alarm. He had really done everything it was possible to do, under the circumstances, handicapped as he had been by a late start. But he hadn't caught the Crow, and it was this distasteful fact which rankled.

It was late afternoon when they broke out of the hills along a small stream and came to a giant cottonwood that grew in a bend of the creek. The tree in itself was conspicuous, but now the official's attention was attracted by a small square of white on its trunk. He knew it was a notice and he also knew there had been no notice there when he had ridden with his men into the hills. He had an instant premonition of its import and spurred his horse toward the tree. He swore as he saw a square sheet of white paper with the crude drawing of a crow upon it. Below were the words:

HOPE YOU HAD A NICE TRIP.

The men about him talked excitedly, but Sheriff Drew remained silent. There was no mistaking who had left the notice. The thing was in keeping with the insolent defiance and atrocious audacity of the Crow. When the sheriff finally spoke, it was in a cool, even voice.

He said: "He must have back trailed on us, or maybe he was hiding out up here watching us when we came. This Crow party is an expert trailer, and, being alone, he could pull stunts that another outlaw, not so smart, with a gang following him, couldn't pull. He hasn't got anybody with him so far as we know, so he must have put this notice up himself."

Drew paused and looked at the interested faces of the men who were listening. "You've got to remember, boys," he went on smoothly, "that we haven't been trailing any common desperado. This Crow doesn't aim to just get out of the way as quick as possible and spend his horse in fast riding. He's too clever for that. It may be my fault in leading you, but it isn't any of your fault that we didn't catch up with him or get a shot at him. If you boys want to … I'm leaving it up to you … I'd just as soon you wouldn't say anything about this notice."

There came a loud murmur of assent from the posse members.

"Thanks, boys," sang the sheriff pleasantly as he dismounted. "Now I'm going to scribble something on this myself, not expecting that anybody will see it, understand? This notice was aimed at me, and if I want to kid myself, I guess I have that right."

He took a soft lead pencil from the left upper pocket of his vest and inscribed on the top of the notice.

Will post an answer here in a week.—Drew

"Just for my own amusement, understand, boys?" he said as he got back into his saddle. "Now we'll breeze for Milton where I'll get plenty from the powers that be. Whether they can make me like it is another question."

He smiled grimly, and his features again betrayed serious thought as they rode away. For once, during his experience as sheriff, Drew was thoroughly worried. He owned a ranch, and he had an enviable reputation for honesty, efficiency, and common sense—the latter tempering his conceptions of justice to no small extent. The violation of Bend County territory by the Crow threatened Drew's reputation as a sheriff. The sheriffs of other counties in the north range would have their eyes upon him to see what he would do. And for his own satisfaction and peace of mind, it was essential that he capture or dispense with the infamous outlaw some way.

When the posse rode into Milton in the early dusk, the sheriff was not in any too pleasant frame of mind. He had formulated no definite plan of campaign against the bandit and had merely outlined the routine preliminaries in his mind. He had a feeling that in some way the Crow would have to be lured into striking again. There was just a chance that the outlaw would get to see what had been written by Drew on the notice posted on the trunk of the big cottonwood tree.

Members of the posse who lived in Milton or nearby struck out for their homes or the ranches where they were employed, and Drew went to the hotel for supper with the deputies and men he had brought from Bend City. He disregarded the talk at the table. He knew three stockmen were waiting for him in the hotel lobby and had been apprised of Sylvester Graham's desire to see him when he had eaten. News of the failure to find the outlaw or get word of his movements had spread through the town until everyone was aware of the situation by the time the sheriff sat down at the table.

The Crow had robbed the Milton Bank and made a clean getaway!

Twenty minutes after he had finished his supper, Sheriff Drew sat in Sylvester Graham's private office in the bank with four others. Behind his broad desk, with the rays of the lamp lighting his strong face, sat Graham. Drew sat at one end of the desk where he could see Graham and the three stockmen—Jim Wessel, Roy Lamby, and Frank Payne, all powerful cattlemen and directors in the bank, as well as prominent in the affairs of the town. Payne was spokesman for the group in his capacity of president of the Stockmen's Association. He was a large man of medium height, clean-shaven, bluff in manner, abrupt and gruff in speech.

Sylvester Graham was speaking in a slow, even voice, keeping his eyes on Sheriff Hal Drew, who was smoking a cigar and not looking at him.

"Your report, then, is that you've been three days on this outlaw's trail without seeing sign of him, Sheriff?"

"Don't even know that I was on his trail," drawled the sheriff.

"Some folks might be apt to say that it doesn't speak well for you, Sheriff," said Graham impatiently, "but I'm not one of them. I *will* say, however, that it speaks well for the bandit."

"He's clever, and he's alone," said Drew calmly. "You'll remember I told you I didn't expect to catch him the first time out." He was looking absently at Payne, who was frowning.

"You seem to take it as a matter of course," Graham snapped out. "It seems to me, and to these gentlemen with whom I've been conferring, that this is a mighty serious business. After all, this is an important bank and it was a high-handed crime."

"A posse should have gone out of this town half an hour after the robbery," said Drew sternly, looking at the banker for the first time. "You've kicked on my placing what you called 'high-priced law' in this town, and you know it. I'm admitting my mistake in listening to you in the first place. I notice you didn't invite the town constable to this meeting."

"Why should I, when we have the sheriff of the county here?" Graham flared.

"I can't perform miracles," replied the sheriff in an acid tone. "In the future I'll have a deputy here, well paid, so he'll be a man who knows his business. But that doesn't concern the matter in hand."

"Certainly not," said Graham icily. "If you'll listen a moment, I'll give you my idea of what our next move should be."

"Suppose you let the sheriff tell what *he* has in mind," Payne put in. "We elected him sheriff and it seems to me that he ought to know what to do. If I thought a bunch of men could catch this Crow, we'd take every man off the range and send 'em out."

"I had to take a chance on the Crow hitting for the high hills," said Drew. "And it's like looking for a needle in a haystack to find one raider who knows his business in the Rocky Mountains. The posse hunt was a first move that had to be made on the chance that it might show something. The next move is simply another preliminary."

"And what is that?" Payne asked curiously.

"The customary offer of a reward," the sheriff answered, inspecting the ash on the end of his cigar before he flicked it on the floor.

"I won't hear of it!" cried Graham. "It's a confession of weakness!"

"Not necessarily," drawled Hal Drew, squinting at the stockmen. "Maybe I know more about this Crow person than you folks do. He's bad medicine anyway you look at him. Killing is the easiest thing he does. He hasn't worked this far northwest before. There are no rewards out for him up here that I know of. There's one thing about a reward … it keeps folks looking and listening. A man who's sure he has the bandit cornered will take a chance quicker with a big reward in sight then he would otherwise. It stimulates individual trailing and trying for one thing. I suppose you'd like to have your twenty thousand odd dollars back, eh, Graham?"

"Whether we get the money back or not, I want that bluffing outlaw," Graham asserted bitterly.

"Don't think for a minute that he's bluffing," said Drew coolly. "If you told him what you said you did, it was because you didn't know the man. If he's bluffing, it's the most dangerous bluff you ever ran up against, take it from me."

"How much reward would you offer?" asked Payne, scowling at the banker. "It wouldn't look any too good if we didn't offer one."

"Make it a good one," the sheriff advised. "Goodness knows I don't want it. In fact, I don't expect any of my men to get it. But some lone hand might get it by bringing the Crow in with a bullet in his back. I reckon we don't care *how* we get him. As you say, Frank, the bank and the county has to put up a front. I'd say make it five thousand from the bank and five thousand from the county." He was thinking of the notice on the cottonwood tree and of the reward poster he would put over it as his answer.

"I'll never agree to it!" declared Graham emphatically.

"On the other hand, Sil," Payne said slowly, "Hal is right. We can't have people saying that the bank is too cheap to even offer a reward." He glanced at the two cattlemen with him and they nodded. "We've pretty near got to offer the reward, and there shouldn't be any reason to call a meeting of the board of directors. There are four of us here and the others will stand by us."

Graham glowered. He knew what Payne meant. If he didn't agree to the offer of the reward, the directors would get together and carry it over his head. "It's not the first time I've had a club held over my head," the banker growled. "If you feel that way about it, it's all right with me, but I'd rather have the county do it." He looked squarely at Sheriff Drew.

"I'll see that the county offers an additional five thousand," Drew said dryly. "It'll give the Crow a laugh anyway. It wouldn't surprise me if he came back to claim it."

"Enough of such nonsense," blurted Graham. "I'll admit that he is a dangerous character. What do you propose to do next, Drew?"

"I am going to go about my duty in the way I best see fit," was the sheriff's dignified reply. "I never discuss my plans outside the men who are going to work with me. I learned that much long ago. I'm going to try to get the Crow."

"Of course," snorted the irate banker. "And I'm going to try, too. As president of this bank, Sheriff, I do not have to depend upon your efforts entirely in the matter of rounding up this criminal. I'm going to send for a man to work on his own in this case." He looked at Payne and the other two stockmen with triumph in his eyes.

"The bank can call for outside help, if it wants to, but the county won't," Drew said mildly. "I'm entitled to know who you've got in mind, Graham. In fact, I've *got* to know."

"We've *all* got to know, for that matter," Payne ejaculated.

"Very well." Graham cleared his throat impressively. "As some of you may know, I have a relative who is president of a bank in the southern part of the state. Last fall he was placed in a position similar to that in which I am placed now. His bank was held up and robbed of twelve thousand dollars by three masked men. The ... er ... county authorities were unable to apprehend the bandits. He sent for a man of whom he had heard, and that man shot and killed one of the outlaws, wounded another, and captured the third, recovering most of the stolen money. I intend to send for that man. His name is Mel Davitt."

The sheriff pursed his lips as Payne looked at him questioningly. "I've heard of Davitt," Drew confessed. "He doesn't work at such things regularly, and he has a peculiar way of working when he does work. He was an Association agent once down Miles City way, and they kicked him out because he let a man go when he rounded up a bunch of rustlers ... with help. He's a gunman, of course, but so is the Crow, for that matter. He's young, too."

"As president of the bank, I'm entitled to try every means to recover the bank's money," said Graham. "I don't want you to think I'm going over your head in this matter, Sheriff Drew, for it really is just an extra precaution. As you said, the bank has the right ..."

"Go ahead and call in your man," Payne interrupted. "One more on the trail won't do any harm, and the sheriff just got through telling you that's what the rewards were for ... to attract man hunters."

"I have absolutely no objections," said the sheriff heartily. "I'll cooperate with him on the side and I want to talk to him when he comes."

"Then our business is settled," Graham declared, rubbing his hands with satisfaction.

Sheriff Drew rose from his chair. "I'm going to Bend City in the morning, but I'll be back maybe tomorrow night. I'll have the reward notices printed. I'm obliged to you, Graham, for your good description of this Crow party. I've got a hunch we'll get him yet."

When he was again alone in his office, Graham penned a note to his banking relative asking him to arrange for the immediate services of Mel Davitt for the State Bank of Milton.

CHAPTER THREE

It was the brilliant hour before sunset, with the prairie running gold, and the trees along the creek an emerald string of beads trailing about the pink and purple buttes. The sky was a lazy blue with a few vagrant white clouds floating like sails becalmed on a listless sea. A breeze was stirring, and meadowlarks chirped in erratic flight. The breath of the earth was warm.

Buck Granger was riding north toward Milton.

More than one girl, new to the north range country, had termed Buck Granger "a typical buckaroo," and a number of them had learned he was much more than that—as almost any man could have told them. He was red-haired, good-looking, splendidly set up, with a daredevil light in his hazel eyes. He was twenty-four and looked it, normally, but when angered, which was seldom, he appeared older and harder, and his lips and eyes lost their boyish devil lights. He was strictly "cow people," as he aptly put it, with a smile.

This late afternoon he was in a happy mood, which was his leading and best-liked characteristic. He shook out his reins and burst into song in as sweet a baritone as the range could boast.

> Lock me in the jail to stay!
> But I'll get outta there any-
>   way!
> I'll squeeze through the bars
>   in broad daylight,
> Or walk out the front in the
>   black midnight!

He swung in closer to the trees along the creek that flowed southward from Milton. His pace would bring him to town for supper. He would be riding back to the big Payne Ranch in the dawn, so he thought. His song swelled on the breeze.

> I won't stay in jail for no
>   lawman;
> Try and keep me there, if
>   you can!
> I'll break off the door and
>   throw it away,
> Before I'll let em' keep me in
>   the jail to stay!

A rider burst out of the trees and raced his horse in close to the singer.

"You figure on going to jail, stranger?" came the challenge in a cheerful voice, accompanied by a flashing smile.

Buck pulled up his horse. "I'm not a stranger, bozo, I live here," he shot back coolly. "That's mistake number one. I don't favor any such introduction as yours for mistake number two. Now, you tell one."

He was neither smiling nor frowning, for the newcomer was plainly a genial sort with range breeding sticking out all over him, as the saying has it. He was probably two, perhaps three years older than Buck, clean-cut as to features, with cool, gray eyes. He had the strong, slim, tapering build of a natural-born rider. He wore a pearl-handled gun in a worn black holster, and as Buck noted it, he took his hand off his own weapon. It was all too apparent that there was nothing hostile about the man or his manner of greeting.

"I might as well make mistake number three," said the rider, his eyes twinkling, "in taking it that you're a cow person."

This was right in Buck's territory and he ventured a grin. "I am that and no mistake," he confessed. "You look like a waddy yourself, although I dunno …" He couldn't quite make the other out.

"If you think of all the cattle you've ever seen," said the stranger gravely, "and then think of all the range you've ever seen and think of all the cattle you've ever seen on all the range you've ever seen, multiplied by all the cattle and range you can think of …"

"I'll know what kind of a cow person you are, I suppose," Buck interpolated with a wide grin. "You working on this range? I don't remember seeing you before."

"You wouldn't." The other nodded. "I don't always look the same and I'm not working on this range … as yet. Mind telling me who you happen to be representing yourself at present?"

"I'm Buck Granger from the Payne Ranch, which ranch has all the cattle you've seen multiplied by all the range you haven't seen skinned by forty sections. What's your alibi when it comes to names? You don't have to tell where you're from unless somebody's chasing you."

"I'm known as the Great-Horned-Toad-from-the-Pecos," was the answer, with the lift of a fine pair of brows. "I spit poison and eat fire. I catch bullets between my teeth and lick 'em. Can you keep a secret, Buck?"

"I haven't told you my middle name," Buck answered. "I'll trade."

"Then call me Mel Davitt, for that's my right name," said the stranger. "I'm from the south, and since I'm new up here, and you look charitably inclined, maybe you'll confirm my suspicions that the town of Milton is north of here, not too far, and, if you're riding that way, let me ride along with you … you to give me all the information I should have on the way." Davitt nodded brightly.

Buck Granger laughed. "I should have spotted your Texas crimp and string to your words. Milton sure is just north of here, and I'm going that way. We can ride along easy and make it just after sundown for a good supper at the Grand Prairie Hotel. You can get anything you can pay for in town and you can get trouble for nothing. A lone worker poked twenty thousand out of the bank up there the other day, but they'd never take you for him. Riding in with me makes you safe and respectable for the time being, so let's jog along."

"You might be taking a chance if you ride along with me to square me off," warned Davitt. They were riding now, and each was eyeing the splendid mount of the other. "You got a fair horse there," said Davitt.

"You're not riding a mule yourself," Buck answered.

"What about this gun-poking at the bank?" asked Davitt.

"Outlaw who calls himself the Crow held it up and beat it for good a week ago," replied Buck. "They want him bad. My boss is a director of the bank, too. Ten thousand reward out for the Crow, so if you're short, there's your chance."

"Let's you and me go out and get him," suggested Davitt.

"Yeah?" Buck shot him a curious look. "Why not? The sheriff can't get within shooting range of him, so we ought to make it easy."

"Going in on ranch business, Buck?" asked Davitt pleasantly.

"Nope, I'm going in to a dance," replied the cowpuncher. "I'm supposed to be back on circle at daylight. What you up here for?"

"I'm up here to make a stake at something," said Davitt. "I've got a white shirt and a tie in my slicker pack, so what's to stop me going to the dance along with you?"

"Nothing … if you've got two dollars. They don't run any cheap dances in Milton and the girls go free. You'd be pretty sure of getting a partner if you can kick your feet."

"Not so sure as you think," said Davitt. "I'd have to dance with the prettiest girl there, if I went."

"I see," Buck said, giving him a quizzical look. "Well, it wouldn't be hard to pick her out. She's Virginia Graham, daughter of old Sylvester Graham, president of the bank and the bozo who holds the keys to all the mortgages. She's particular who she dances with, but you give her that horned-toad stuff. She'd be liable to fall for that." Buck laughed heartily.

"I suppose you know her," Davitt conjectured, ignoring Buck's joke and laughter.

"Sure, I know her. I'm good for a dance if she feels like it. Listen, I'm telling you a lot of things, but I'm not adopting you or anything like that. I'm just riding along with you, understand?"

"I gather this Virginia lady is plumb high-toned," was Davitt's comment. "And if you adopted me, you'd have something on your hands, boy. I can streak it for town if my company is bothering you any."

Buck frowned. "I didn't mean that exactly. But I don't know you and that's a fact if it isn't anything else. I don't reckon I ought to be talkin' to you about Miss Virginia, but I warn you she doesn't dance around promiscuous with strangers."

"That's fair. Well, Buck, there's nothing wrong with me. I haven't been to a dance in a long time. I'd like to go tonight. If Miss Virginia requires it, why don't you take a chance and introduce me?"

Buck Granger looked startled. "Why … well, we'll see."

"I'll be doggoned if you're not afraid of her!" exclaimed Davitt.

Buck's face reddened with anger. "You're fresh, bozo," he said.

"You just think so," returned Davitt with a cool look. "I've watched you riding along for two or three miles. I formed an opinion of you before I busted out from the trees. I can tell a little about a man even by the way he rides. I heard your song and saw the look in your eyes, and read your face, and decided you were foursquare. So you see, it was me who invited this ride and not you who did the inviting. I don't make up with every stranger I see coming along any more than you do. And there's no use in getting mad at me, because it won't do you any good."

Buck had been studying the other as he listened. Here was no cowhand, he decided. Perhaps he was the son of a rancher on the southern ranges somewhere. Buck was handicapped in that he knew nothing of the country south of the Missouri. But Mel Davitt was not a common cowpuncher, and he didn't look like a professional gambler, and one look into his eyes convinced Buck that his new acquaintance was not a shady character. Since Payne had made no mention to anyone that Sylvester Graham was sending for an operative from outside the county to help hunt down the Crow, word could not have got to Buck that such a man was coming. And even if he had known, there was absolutely nothing about Davitt's appearance to suggest that he might be the man. Buck concluded that it was because Davitt talked a little better than the average cowhand that he seemed different.

"You've had quite a bit of schooling, haven't you?" he asked.

"From reading, boy," replied Davitt with a friendly smile. "I've always been a hand to read. I had a kid's schooling before I had to go to work. The rest of it I got by reading everything I could get my hands on. Man, I've read *The Rise and Fall of the*

Roman Empire!" He lifted his brows and emphasized his words with nods of his head and a gleam of triumph came into his eyes.

Buck grinned broadly. "I suppose you don't have much time to read things like playing cards, though," he remarked.

"I can shut my eyes after seeing my hole card and play better stud than you ever heard a gambler lie about," was the answer.

Buck laughed this time. "I guess you're all right," he sang. "I'll take a chance on you. C'mon, Mel, the town's straight ahead."

They let out their horses and raced at tremendous speed toward the town that now showed dimly in its setting of trees in a bend of the creek less than two miles away. The sun dropped behind the peaks and the high western sky swam in crimson glory as they slowed their pace and cantered into the dust of Milton's main street.

CHAPTER FOUR

When they had put up their horses, and Mel Davitt had tossed the liveryman a gold piece with the admonition to "treat my horse like he was your own brother," they started for the hotel. Davitt was carrying his slicker pack, having explained that it contained certain articles of wearing apparel that he might need.

"I'm going to get a room and wash up before supper," he told Buck. "Maybe they'll have the means of a bath here. I'm sick of river water with my shirt for a towel. If you want to use my room for anything, like combing your hair or such, you're welcome."

"Get your room and doll yourself up and I'll meet you in the bar," said Buck. "I might leave my shooting iron up there during the dance, and I might leave it with the clerk downstairs. I'll see you later."

"Well put." Davitt smiled. "You're not dumb, Buck. Why didn't you come right out and say that guns are barred at the dance? I know you're not going to leave yours with me any more than I'd leave mine with you. Maybe I'll hide mine behind the piano."

"They don't stand for any rough stuff at social affairs here," said Buck pointedly, as they went up the steps and entered the small lobby. "I'll be in the first door to the right of the hall there."

When Davitt appeared in the bar nearly an hour later, Buck caught himself looking at his new acquaintance in astonishment and admiration. It was vividly apparent that Davitt had bathed and was refreshed as a result. He was clean-shaven, wore a clean, light blue shirt of finest thin broadcloth, a dark blue four-in-hand, gray trousers with their bottoms over the tops of brilliantly polished riding boots. The freedom from cartridge belt and gun accentuated the slim waist of his superb figure.

"You'll do," said Buck with a pleased expression. "You look good enough to be introduced around to the boys. Where'd you get the big-town pants?"

"The Prince of Wales sends me a duplicate of everything he wears, son," was Davitt's lofty reply. "I don't feel like meeting any of the boys till I've had supper. You eat yet ... or are you waiting for me to do the honors before we take what they've got left?"

"How about yourself?" Buck asked, pushing away his empty beer glass.

"Don't feel like it," was the crisp answer. "Let's go in."

They didn't talk about much of anything during the meal. The twilight had deepened into night in the small dining room and the lamps had been lighted. Outside, the last pale light of the sunset's afterglow still lingered when they went into the street.

Mel Davitt and Buck attracted more than a passing glance from those they met. They were of equal height and of almost identical build. Cowpunchers singled them out as expert riders at a glance. More than one girl who spoke to Buck threw Davitt a single glance, but Buck volunteered no introduction.

A tall man who would have attracted attention most anywhere came around the corner as they reached the bank. Like others, he nodded to Buck and looked at Davitt keenly. Then he stopped to speak to Buck.

"Frank Payne told me he was going to pay you off with your dance ticket one of these times," he said in a bantering voice.

"I've special permission this time from the wagon boss," Buck said, grinning. "The old man ain't got anything against me. Oh, Sheriff, this is Mister … *er* … Davey." He turned to Davitt, who didn't bother to correct the name. "This is Sheriff Hal Drew," he said by way of introduction.

"How do you do," said Davitt, taking the sheriff's proffered hand. There was nothing in the official's gaze to indicate that he suspected his identity.

"Another Payne buckaroo, eh?" Drew commented amiably. "Well, you two make a pair. They're tuning up over at the dance hall, so I won't be taking more of your time. Don't step on anybody's toes, Buck."

"*Humph*," Buck said as they walked on. "He thinks I'm a trouble omen. He's up here on that robbery business. There's the bank over on that corner. Brand new and shining like a target. Reckon this Crow outlaw just couldn't pass it up."

Davitt looked at the bank with interest. "They don't make 'em strong enough to stop a first-class hold-up man," he commented.

They went on to the dance hall, which was over a general store. The dance was already in progress and Davitt told Buck to go ahead and dance while he got his bearings with the spectators grouped about the door. He watched Buck cross the floor to where three girls were sitting in chairs along the wall with some fellows standing about them. When the orchestra struck up he saw Buck emerge with a dark-haired girl with dancing eyes and laughing lips. He didn't have to look hard to know that this was Buck's favorite among the girls present, and that she was glad to be dancing with him. Then he studied the couples on the floor, noting the girls particularly. At last he saw her.

She was dancing with a tall youth whose face lacked the depth of tan that it would have shown had he been on the range the whole year round. Either he was from a large town or city, or he had been away to school. Davitt was inclined to the last thought because of his dress. He had scant time for the girl's partner, however, for Virginia Graham's hair, of the color of burnished copper, her dark eyes, her softly curved lips, her poise of graceful, lissome body, easily marked her as the most beautiful girl there. He was sure she was the girl Buck had spoken of the moment he set his eyes on her. He was not sorry he had come to the dance, for it was worth it just to see Virginia.

Buck came along two dances later, and Davitt drew him aside.

"Who's that girl sitting over there with the tall fellow in town clothes?" Davitt asked. "The one with the head of hair, I mean. I saw you speak to her, but I don't blame you for sticking close to the snuggly little one you favor. She's your type. I'd like for to meet the one with the hair."

"Oh, yeah?" said Buck sarcastically. "Just like that, huh? So you spotted her. Who wouldn't? That's Virginia Graham, of course. Who'd think that old money-grabbing iceberg could have a daughter like that. The gentleman ... get the word ... who's with her is Chester Wessel. He's just finished college somewhere in the East. His old man owns one of our biggest ranches. He's probably read the rise and fall of *all* the empires, not just Rome, or whatever you said it was. I don't reckon he'd want her dancing with any horned toads."

Davitt grasped Buck's arm and squeezed it until the cow-puncher winced. "I want to meet her," he hissed in Buck's ear. "All you've got to say is just ... 'this is Mister Davitt who wants to meet you' ... see? I'll do the rest."

Buck placed both hands on his hips and looked at him. "Well now, ain't that easy? Just as smooth as glass. That's all I have to say, eh? Well, Mister Horned-Toad, you come right along, and I'll do just as you say. Later I can tell her I did it on a bet or something and explain you got her wrong and I wanted to see you set right. Come right along with me."

He led Davitt across the floor and into the group surrounding the girl. "Miss Graham, this is Mister Devitt, who wants to meet you," he introduced sweetly.

Virginia Graham arched her pretty brows a trifle. "How do you do, Mister Devitt," she said in a conventional voice.

"Quite well," said Davitt with a credible bow. "Buck, here, means Davitt, since his E carries the Greek accent." He was quick to see her eyes light with interest and noted Chester Wessel was frowning.

"Mister Davitt," explained Buck politely, "is a horned toad from Texas." He bowed and smiled.

"Which naturally explains everything," Davitt said, nodding with a smile. His smile was catching, and everyone smiled faintly except Wessel. "I came all the way up here to ask you for the honor and enjoyment of dancing with you, Miss Graham," said Davitt with a challenge in his eyes.

At this moment the orchestra began playing.

"I believe *I* have this, Virginia," Wessel declared, touching her arm.

"Oh, you can let it go, Chester," said the girl. "I believe I'll dance with Mister Davitt. Horned toads from Texas are such a novelty."

"What you told him squelched him plenty, Miss Virginia," said Davitt as they swung out on the floor.

She found out at once that he was an excellent dancer. "I believe you misunderstood the nature of my remark, Mister Davitt," she said with dignity. "It is not necessary to squelch Mister Wessel and what you said was rather rude."

"I'm sorry, but I hope Chet Wessel won't begrudge me this dance, Miss Virginia. It is more of a pleasure than you think, and I am very grateful."

"That's a pretty little speech," said Virginia. "How did you learn my first name?"

"I took care to make discreet inquiries the moment I set eyes on you," he said in her ear. "It goes without saying that you are easily the glorious star among the girls present, although that may sound commonplace. I'm going further afield, Miss Virginia. You are one of the most beautiful young women … you're more than a girl … that I ever saw, and I've covered considerable territory. I bullied Buck Granger into our introduction and I can't remember offhand that I ever did such a thing before."

"I'll have to accept the compliment, Mister Davitt," Virginia said, and smiled. "After all, Chester Wessel has told me the same thing." She was pleased, nevertheless, and he sensed it.

"Chet has been away to school, hasn't he?" asked Davitt politely.

"He graduated this spring from the University of Minnesota," was the girl's reply.

"Oh, yes. Agricultural, isn't it? By the way, did he ever mention that he had read *The Rise and Fall of the Roman Empire?*"

"Why, no," she answered with a quick look of surprise.

"Well, *I* have read it," Davitt announced. "I've had to depend upon books for my education, mostly. I knew the instant I saw you that you would have a pretty name and I can't help calling you Miss Virginia. Rear names are often so common."

"Yours isn't so common, Mister Davitt. I've never heard it but once before."

"Was it a hanging?" He arched his brows.

Virginia indulged in an undignified giggle, then flushed as she realized it. "You don't talk so bad," she said in a patronizing tone. "And you don't look so terrible."

"I always try to dress, and look, and talk my best when in such company," he told her stiffly.

"For a man of your … *ah* … profession, I should have expected to meet a much rougher character," she said. "To be perfectly frank with you, Mister Davitt, I decided to dance with you because I was interested."

"In me or in what you call my profession?" he asked quickly.

"I've never met a professional man hunter before," she replied slowly. "If you are the man I think you are, I will tell you that the only time I heard the name before tonight was when my father told me he was expecting a man of that name to do some … some work for him." She was looking at him closely as the music came to a stop.

"In that case, you will perhaps talk with me a little," he said. "I don't believe I care to dance with any other girl tonight. Let's go to the refreshment booth and have a cool soda or lemonade."

They took their tall glasses out on a small balcony at the side of the hall near the rear. A breeze was whispering in the cottonwoods, and the starlight, filtering through the branches, scattered diamonds among the trees. Several other couples were on the balcony, standing close, talking in subdued tones with occasional ripples of laughter.

"You are the daughter, then, of Graham, the banker?" Davitt asked pleasantly. "By banker do you mean faro or mortgages?"

"I'll overlook that thrust, Mister Davitt," the girl retorted with a trace of anger in her voice. "My father is the president of the bank in Milton, and he is generally respected."

"No doubt," Davitt said with a shrug. "My father banked faro and was killed because he stuck to a square box. There are different kinds of banking, of course." He saw Virginia bite her lip as if she regretted her hasty speech, although he had given her just cause to be irritated. "Did your father say why he had sent for me?"

"So you are the man!" She looked at him curiously. "He said he expected you to hunt down the outlaw they call the Crow who robbed the bank. He told me not to tell anyone, and I don't believe anyone knows, outside of mother and me and a few of the bank directors and the sheriff. Your coming is supposed to be something of a secret."

"It still is, unless you give me away, Miss Virginia. No one knows me up here. I met Buck Granger riding in. He only knows my name. Still, I don't usually work in secret."

"You seem young for such a dangerous business," she observed.

"And your conjectures seem too mature for your years," he responded. "I didn't intend to interject that angle of myself ... my personality ... into our talk. You know I have to make a living."

She drew away from him just enough so that her move was perceptible. "Will you pardon me if I ask you if you are what they call a paid gunman?" she said rather timidly.

He laughed. "When I sell my services, my gun goes along with 'em," he answered. "What you really wanted to ask me is if I'm what they call a killer, isn't that about it?"

"I understand you have had to ... to ..." She couldn't get the word out as she caught the look in his eyes.

"Yes ... to prevent being killed myself," he supplied. "In a way it isn't a business with me, although I charge plenty. I think I'll accept this assignment out of pure deviltry."

"Deviltry?" Virginia's surprise showed plainly in her eyes.

"Yes," said Davitt soberly. "I'm anxious to match wits with the Crow. He's dangerous and he's clever. I'd rather match wits with him than match guns. In either case, I think it would be a fifty-fifty match."

Virginia decided she liked his eyes best when he was serious. For that matter he was dangerously good-looking, and he did

have an interesting personality. She spurned the idea that his profession, as she thought of it, might appeal to her romantic fancy.
But he fascinated her, in a way, and she found herself thrilling at
the thought.

"I suppose the nature of your business makes an impression
on the girls you meet," she said, and instantly regretted her words.

"Not if I can help it," he said. "Usually they ... don't know."

"Then you're not proud of it?" she hastened to say.

"Is your sheriff proud of his job?" asked Davitt tartly.

"I suppose I don't know what I'm talking about, Mister
Davitt. It's the words *man hunter* which I don't like. Father used it
as if you should be held in awe. You don't seem so fearful to me."

"I thank you for saying that, Miss Virginia."

Davitt turned as a man came up to them and saw Chester
Wessel.

"Really, Virginia, I gave up the last dance," Wessel said, with a
cool look at Davitt. "Unless you want to miss this one ..."

"Why don't you introduce me to your friend, Miss Virginia?"
said Davitt, smiling at the girl.

Virginia hesitated while Wessel frowned as if he had been af-
fronted. "This is Mister Davitt, Mister Wessel," she said hurriedly.

"Pleased to meet you," Wessel said, extending a cold hand.

"You naturally would be," said Davitt, gripping the hand in
fingers of steel. "How's the cow business up in these parts?"

"It's better than no business at all," Wessel snapped. "If you're
ready, Virginia, we'll go in and dance."

"Go right ahead, Miss Virginia." Davitt nodded affably. "I'll
see you again, of course."

The girl gave him a stare, and then turned away with Wessel,
without speaking, and joined the couples who were leaving the
balcony.

Davitt finished his drink alone, his eyes coolly contemplative as he gazed through the branches at the starlit sky. He put his empty glass beside Virginia's on the balcony rail and rolled and lighted a cigarette while the dance went on within the hall. He had hardly time for two or three puffs when Buck Granger joined him.

"How'd you make out?" asked the cowpuncher. "What'd you say to Chet Wessel? He's dancing with Miss Virginia and his face is chiseled into a terrible scowl. Looks like he's arguing with her, but it isn't getting him anything, if I'm any judge."

"He would do that," said Davitt thoughtfully. "He's that kind."

"Well, if you've decided to woo and win the gal, don't let any worry about Chet keep you awake nights," drawled Buck. "He hasn't been around much the last few years and he calls her by her first name because he went to school with her. You've got clear sailing, if you've got money and also social position somewhere besides in Texas."

Davitt chuckled. "I like you, Buck, because you've got a sense of humor," he said, sobering.

"I'd sure need it if I traveled with you much," was Buck's comeback. "Anyway, you had the grand dame listening and that's a start."

"Maybe that's all it will be," mused Davitt. He looked out on the dance floor and plucked at Buck's arm. "Look, they've stopped dancing. Who's that bull they're talking with?"

Buck looked and smiled broadly. "That's the keeper of the mortgages and no less," he announced. "I reckon he'll be looking you up. Well, it looks like a warm summer, Mel, old boy. I'll see you later." With this, Buck swung over the balcony rail, grasped one of the supports, and dropped lightly to the ground, leaving Davitt alone.

CHAPTER FIVE

Davitt studied the banker from the shadow of the balcony. He had been told by Graham's relative that the man was powerful, a clever and capable financier, firm in support of his own opinions, bold and unchangeable in his decisions. He had a strong face, and his clear, cold eyes impressed Davitt most.

Sylvester Graham and his daughter sat down on the opposite side of the hall from the balcony and Chester Wessel started in Davitt's direction. Davitt muttered something in an annoyed tone, and then followed Buck's example by swinging over the balcony rail and dropping to the ground. But this was merely to avoid Wessel, for Davitt walked around to the front steps that lead to the hall. Here he hesitated, considering the advisability of returning to the dance floor to ask Virginia Graham for another dance later in the evening. He pondered the matter just long enough to permit Graham to conclude his talk with his daughter. He heard a heavy tread on the stairs and turned just in time to meet the banker's eyes as the latter looked up and down the street. But Graham must have recognized him in the brief glance by the description Virginia had undoubtedly given him.

He strode up to Davitt. "Is your name Davitt?" he asked.

Davitt bristled instantly at the tone of the banker's voice. What was more, the look in Graham's eyes was not precisely one of welcome.

"It might be," he answered coldly. "It would depend to some extent on who wanted to know."

"No doubt," grunted Graham. "Huh, I am Sylvester Graham, president of the State Bank of Milton, and if you're the Davitt I'm thinking of, it was your duty to report to me immediately on arrival."

"I came here to see a man named Graham," drawled Davitt, "and he is a banker. But I don't usually report for the first time after business hours."

There was disapproval in Graham's eyes. "I'm the man you were to report to, I expect," he said crisply. "You heard my name. Have you a letter addressed to me?"

"Why, yes ... now that I think of it," replied Davitt. He brought a sealed envelope from the inside pocket of his coat and handed it to the banker. "These are my credentials. I happen to know you're Graham, or I wouldn't hand them over so easy."

"I have an appointment with Sheriff Drew," said Graham tartly, taking the envelope. "Suppose you go along with me to see him."

"I can spare half an hour," Davitt said dryly.

It was a matter of minutes before Graham, Drew, and Davitt were seated in Graham's private office in the bank.

"Do you make a practice of transacting business in this office at night?" asked Davitt, after the banker had formally introduced him to Sheriff Drew.

"It is the only office I use," Graham snapped. "Isn't it good enough?" It was not for personal reasons that he disapproved of Davitt almost at first sight.

"Nice office," said Davitt, "but it seems dangerous to me for you to be going in and out of the bank at night. Suppose somebody followed you going in or stopped you going out?"

"*Humph*," grunted the banker with a look at the sheriff. "No one comes in or goes out of here except on business. I look out for that, young man."

"Well, the Crow had business here and that's a fact," Davitt observed.

Graham's face darkened while the sheriff looked at Davitt with new interest. "That remark was uncalled for," he said. "Youth isn't able to distinguish between a joke and an impertinence. Your credentials are all right, but I'm not sure you're the man for this case."

"You want to be sure before you engage me," said Davitt. "There are certain rigid stipulations that I make before I undertake a case."

Sylvester stared at him. "Such as what?" he blurted.

"For one thing I require a retainer fee," said Davitt pleasantly. "That is usually a first preliminary." He took out the materials for making a smoke.

"You want to be paid in advance?" gasped Graham.

"Partly." Davitt smiled as he rolled a cigarette. "Enough to show good faith on the part of my employer. Who would I be working for in this case ... the bank or the county?"

"Both!" Graham exploded.

"The bank," the sheriff corrected.

"In which case I should have to have a thousand dollars before I took much interest," Davitt announced, striking a match on the bottom of his chair.

"That settles it!" exclaimed Graham. "I pay no man in advance. Why, there's ten thousand dollars reward offered for the Crow, dead or alive."

"That wouldn't do me any good if I was to be found dead instead of the Crow," said Davitt coolly. "I've made considerable money at this business, if you want to call it that, by operating strictly on a business basis. That should appeal to you." He nodded gravely at the banker who sat as if stupefied.

"And what do you guarantee in return for the thousand dollars?" asked the sheriff curiously.

"To start to work in my own way within twelve hours and to clean up the matter as soon as possible, if possible," was the answer.

"Business!" snorted Graham. "Do you call it businesslike to pick up with an irresponsible cowpuncher on your way to town and then go to a frivolous … to a dance before you even report to the people who were thinking of acquiring your services?"

"Were thinking, do you say? If you've given up the idea, there's no sense in my taking up any more of my time here." Davitt rose. "Of course, I shall have to charge you with my expense in coming here, since you sent for me."

"Sit down!" roared Graham, pounding the desk with his right fist. He cooled as Davitt resumed his chair. "This is preposterous," he said, fussing with some odd papers and straightening the ink stand on his desk. He turned to Sheriff Hal Drew. "You've had experience with range operatives, have you not? Does this fellow impress you as a man who could get the Crow?" His lips tightened as he put the question.

"Why not?" the sheriff countered blandly.

"I'll tell you why not," Graham said, frowning at Davitt. "In the first place, he's too young. This Crow is a seasoned outlaw and a desperate man … a killer, in fact. When he pulled his gun in here and I called him a blackguard and a thief and a murderer, he passed over it like so much water running downhill. He makes no pretense of being anything else. He …"

"Did you know just how bad he was when you called him those names?" Davitt interrupted.

"No man can come in here and rob my bank without getting my opinion of him!" thundered Graham.

"Well, he got about seven thousand dollars a word for what you called him," drawled Davitt, "so I reckon he figured he could afford to pass over it for the time being. But you're luckier than you think, because you don't know just how bad the Crow can be."

"I suppose you ought to know," Graham said sarcastically. "Have you ever met him?"

"Oh, I've played cards with him," replied Davitt, offhand.

"You hear that, Sheriff?" Graham said to Hal Drew. "He's run around with such fellows. That's why he wants a thousand in advance. He'll take the money and light out and we'll never see him again. Later on, he'll probably tell this very outlaw about the trick he played." He glared at Davitt. "So far as the bank is concerned, I'm through."

"Well, I'm not," Davitt said, with an icy edge to his voice. "You opened your mouth too wide just now to suit me. It just happens that I didn't know the Crow at the time I played cards with him and you asked me if I had seen him. That's a sizable charge you just made, and I can prove it by the sheriff. I have something of a reputation for being on the square. If I just wanted a thousand dollars, I'd charge you that sum for coming up here, and I'd get it. He paused long enough to nod and gaze a few moments at the banker from between narrowed lids.

"You might as well tell the sheriff all of it," he went on, with a glance at Drew. "You're sore because I busted into that dance, got an introduction to your daughter, brushed young Chet Wessel aside, and danced with her. Whatever she told you, I don't know, but you don't want to let any social ambitions warp your business judgment. I always keep the social side separate from the business side."

Sylvester Graham became red in the face and sputtered in an effort to speak—something the sheriff never had seen him do before.

"Suppose we leave the social side out of it," suggested Drew with a twinkle in his eyes. "After all, Sil, you sent for this man and it's up to you to try him out, now that you have him here. He could charge you a thousand and you'd have to pay it because you could not give any legitimate excuse for not trying him out, and you wouldn't want any publicity. Maybe Davitt is smarter than you think."

"Yes … cheap smartness," jeered the banker. "I know the kind. He shows it by bringing my daughter's name into it."

"That was merely to give you a warning," Davitt said quickly. "You accused me of intending to get a thousand dollars out of you and pocket the money without doing anything for it. That wasn't very broad-minded. As a matter of fact, I might get this man who calls himself the Crow. I can call myself the Canary, and in some ways a canary is smarter than a crow. What you expected to see when you sent for me was an hombre in a black sateen shirt, with fierce whiskers, tobacco juice on his chin, and two six-guns strapped on. I wouldn't be surprised but what the Crow looked too slick to you to be very bad."

Graham controlled his anger this time. "I can't see that you used very much headwork in coming here and giving out your right name at the start," he said, eyeing the sheriff. "If you've got a reputation like you say, the Crow probably has heard of you and the word could get to him that you're here. He has likely heard about the rewards we've offered, and he might link your presence up here to them."

"He might." Davitt nodded, smiling faintly. "I wish you'd tell me just who knew I was coming outside of your immediate family."

The sheriff looked at the banker quickly as he heard this.

"My family never divulges any business I might speak about by chance," said Graham, clearing his throat. "Why, the sheriff, here, knew I sent for you, and so did Frank Payne, Jim Wessel, and Roy Lamby, stockmen and directors of the bank."

"And if those last three let something slip by chance, it might be pretty generally known by this time that I'm here, or on my way," observed Davitt dryly.

"If you were to set out to hunt this outlaw, how would you go about it?" Graham asked, frowning to conceal his curiosity.

"Well, let's see," Davitt said, looking up at the ceiling. "The Crow flies in and taps the bank. You know the old saying … 'Straight as the crow flies.' In this case, the crow flies west. The big mountains are in the west and there are plenty of hiding places in them. You would naturally think he'd go there, wouldn't you? Whether you think so or not, there's your answer and your clue."

The sheriff was listening closely. He now started to speak but thought better of it and looked at Graham who was frankly puzzled.

"There isn't much sense to that answer," said the banker.

"And there wouldn't be much sense in my telling you how I would go about getting the Crow." Davitt smiled. "It might sound downright foolish to you. And I would certainly be a fool to tell you since you are not hiring me. Oh, don't worry. I'm not going to charge you a single cent."

"I don't know, Sil, but that it might be a good idea to let him take a crack at it," said the sheriff to Graham. "Maybe …"

"That's it!" Graham ejaculated. "There's too much maybe to it. I won't say anything behind a man's back that I wouldn't say to his face, and I'll tell you flatly, Davitt, that I don't think you're capable. I'm going to have my way around this bank in this matter, and I'm not hiring you. If you want to nick me for what you call expenses, go to it."

"You've got your own way, mister," said Davitt with a strange cheerfulness in his tone. "I'm not working for you. I take it there wouldn't be any argument about who you would pay the reward money to if it was necessary to pay it."

"There are no strings tied to the reward," Graham said curtly.

Mel Davitt rose abruptly and turned a questioning eye on the sheriff. "I suppose I can have a few words with you, Sheriff, when you're not particularly busy?" he asked. "Later tonight, perhaps?"

"Sure thing," Drew said. "I didn't send for you, but I didn't exactly kick about it, either. If you're going out on your own hook to try and grab these rewards, why, that's what I got 'em offered for. I'll assist anybody anytime to help catch an outlaw in my territory."

"I'll let you out," Graham said, rising briskly. "I wish to speak with the sheriff alone."

"I'll be at the hotel in an hour," said Drew.

Davitt left the bank without speaking further. He walked up the street toward the dance hall and met Buck Granger who was with Chester Wessel. Davitt wondered if Wessel was aware of his identity, not that he especially cared. The two stopped talking as he reached them, and Wessel stepped forward.

"I didn't say quite all I had in mind out there on the balcony," he began. "I ..."

"Forget the rest of it," Davitt broke in sharply. "There's no use in you trying to pick trouble with me, Wessel, because I'm not going to let you do it ... for your own good. You're sore because I danced with a certain young lady tonight, but when you think it over hard enough, you'll see that it wasn't any of your business. You can take that for your end of it."

"Oh, I'm not going to pick trouble with a gunfighter," Wessel said, his face darkening, "but I'm letting you know that you can't bust into this range and run away with anything, even if you are a horned-toad from Texas." His tone carried the inflection of a sneer.

"I'm not packing a gun, as you can see," Davitt said coolly, "but you can start the swiftest fistfight you were ever in with just one more remark like that."

Buck Granger saw the anger flame in Wessel's eyes and he grasped the youth's right arm. "Don't be that foolish," he warned. "I'm saying that Davitt's all right, so lay off. Hallo! Here comes my old man."

Davitt and Wessel both turned and saw a large man, wearing a stockman's hat, approaching with long strides.

"It's Frank Payne," said Wessel. "He'll be looking for you, Buck. I'm going back to the dance." He gave Davitt a dark glance. "I think you're a bluff," he said, as he whirled on his heel.

"Thinking and proving are two different things, Chet!" Davitt called after him.

Frank Payne stopped before them, looking Davitt up and down and then centering his scowling gaze on Buck. "Got your spurs off again, eh?" he said coldly. "Well, my pretty buckaroo, you're through dancing on my time. Don't tell me you got leave to come to town because *I'm* saying when one of my men can leave the ranch. I'll pay you off at the hotel in the morning."

"Oh, there's no hurry," Buck said, flushing. "I can get it any time. I'd rather drop around for it when I go broke."

"That'll be soon enough," Payne snapped. "I'll leave it at the bank. You've set one last bad example." He was looking at Davitt now. "Where you from?" he demanded.

"I'm from Texas," replied Davitt. "Rode up here for the dance."

Payne's face darkened. "Another cowhand who ..."

"I just met up with him today and he's all right," Buck broke in.

"Anybody's all right with you so long as he isn't working and is ready to celebrate," said Payne sternly. "You'd pick up with anybody that came along. I can't stand for it, Buck. You'll have to look for a new job."

"You could have said that in the first place and left the rest of it out," Buck responded in a tone of resentment.

"And you could have left me out, too," Davitt said coolly.

"We're not feeling any too kindly toward strangers right now, in case you haven't heard," Payne shot back. "You'd better watch your step."

"Oh, I've heard," drawled Davitt, "and it looks to me as if somebody slipped long before I got here."

Payne was looking hard at him. "What I said goes," he snapped. Davitt returned his look but didn't offer to answer. Payne flashed another glance at Buck, plainly suspicious, and then strode away.

"Looks like he kicked your job out from under you," Davitt observed.

"It isn't the first time," Buck said, biting his lip. "I had no idea he was in town. Guess he's up here on that bank business. I'll drift back to work in three or four days and he won't say a word."

"Will you take a chance on five thousand dollars or ... a bullet?" Davitt asked, in a businesslike tone.

"I'll take a chance on the five thousand, but not on a bullet," Buck retorted, with a shrug of irritation.

"That's fair enough." Davitt nodded. "Always get your bullet in ahead of the other fellow's, Buck, without taking too much of a chance. Let's go up to my room and I'll tell you a story."

"If it's about the falling down of the Roman empire, I'll need a drink first," said Buck sarcastically.

"It may be about the rising of Buck Granger's star," Davitt said mysteriously. "Come along and hear it, and you'll probably need a drink afterward." He took Buck's arm and turned him toward the hotel. "Let's step right along, for I have an appointment with the sheriff in an hour."

CHAPTER SIX

An hour after daybreak next morning, Mel Davitt and Buck Granger were in the foothills west of Milton. Buck was leading a pack horse laden with camping equipment. To all appearances here were two cowpunchers heading into the mountains for a fishing trip. Buck had secured the pack animal and the equipment after his talk with Davitt in the latter's room, while Davitt had talked with the sheriff in the quiet seclusion of the hotel's front parlor and then had waited for him upstairs.

After entering the hills, they had talked loudly to each other, their remarks pertaining to fishing streams, distances, and the banter of two range hands out on a stolen holiday. But now Buck called to Davitt in a serious tone.

"There's notices on that big cottonwood ahead. We want to give 'em the once-over for they may be rules and regulations. This is forest reserve we're in now and sometimes they're strict. It's probably about being careful with fires."

They pulled up their horses and inspected the notices on the trunk of the tree.

"Somebody's drawn a bird and wrote … 'hope you had a nice

trip,'" said Buck as he surveyed the paper fixed to the tree by the outlaw.

"And somebody's scribbled that he'll answer it in a week," said Davitt loudly. "Hello! The other notice is the answer." He read:

$10,000 REWARD

THE STATE BANK OF MILTON WILL PAY $5,000
AND BEND COUNTY WILL PAY $5,000 IN ADDITION,

FOR THE OUTLAW

THE CROW

WHETHER HE BE DEAD OR ALIVE,

FOR THE ROBBERY OF THE STATE BANK OF MILTON,
BEND COUNTY.

THIS MAN IS SHORT, SLIM, WITH DARK SKIN AND BLACK
EYES THAT STAMP HIM FOR A KILLER AT SIGHT.

SHERIFF HAL DREW
BEND CITY

On the bottom margin of the notice was printed with pen and ink:

A big price for crow meat.—Drew

"Must be that bank robbery business we heard about," Davitt told Buck in a tone that carried clearly. "The top one was left by the fellow who did it, and the bottom one is from the sheriff. Hot chance of this Crow seeing the sheriff's answer. I'll bet he's spending that money in Calgary up in Canada right now."

"And if he isn't, he's a blame fool!" Buck exclaimed.

After some such comment they rode on. Buck was leading the way up the narrow trail, higher and higher into the hills, with Davitt following behind the pack horse. But Buck was looking for sign in the trail ahead and Davitt was stealthily shooting glances behind and to either side. They spoke few words now, for the going was hard and their attention was claimed repeatedly by bad spots in the trail.

Two hours later they halted in a cool ravine that had widened almost to the extent of a valley. There was a clump of trees along a little stream with a large space of meadow about. Here they could not be surprised by the sudden appearance of anyone and their words would not carry to the timber on the slopes.

Buck took the packs off the loaded horse and they hobbled their mounts. While Davitt made a fire and started the coffee, Buck caught some trout for their late breakfast. It didn't take long before they were eating.

"Now our work is all cut out for us," Davitt told Buck, after a period during which he appeared to be preoccupied with his thoughts.

"Well, I don't know just what your work is, but I'm here to look after the horses and the camp and do what other chores you want done at five dollars a day and keep," Buck said, with a nod of his head.

"You looked hard enough at that notice back there to see that the bank is offering five thousand for the Crow and the county is putting up another five thousand, didn't you?" asked Davitt quietly.

"I couldn't help reading what was there in front of my eyes," Buck said, frowning. "But so far as getting this Crow is concerned, it can't be done. I told you so last night when I agreed to come along and guide you through the country and play a part like you suggested. So far as I'm concerned, this is all monkey play, except that I'm earnin' more money with you than I could earn on a ranch and ain't kicking."

"You can have the county's five thousand, Buck," said Davitt cheerfully. "I'll take the bank's."

"Yeah?" jeered Buck. "And how'll you have it?"

"In hundred-dollar notes, Mister Sylvester, if you have 'em, or in anything else that's the equivalent of the sum total," was Davitt's smiling answer. "I hope he asks me that question, Buck, for that's just what I'd tell him."

There was a glimmer of suspicion in Buck's eyes. "Are you sure you're all right in the head?" he said. "I wouldn't take a chance in the hills with a crazy man alone."

Davitt laughed. "If I were crazy, you wouldn't be alone with me in these hills, Buck. I'd be willing to make a strong bet ... if I could expect to prove it ... that we're being watched right this minute."

"By an owl, maybe," said Buck irritably

"By the Crow himself, probably," Davitt said soberly.

Buck looked at him in disgust. He was not in good humor this morning, anyway. He hadn't liked the way Frank Payne had talked to him the night before, and, while he had permission to go to the dance, he didn't feel quite right about going. "You talk like a kid," he said.

Davitt's look sharpened. "When I joined up with you down on the prairie below Milton, I thought you looked a little brighter than the average cow waddy," he said with a hard ring to his voice. "If you are just dumb, I can't afford to have you with me at any price, and five dollars a day is so much bird feed. I told you I was going out after the Crow and that's what I'm here for. Now, if you've got any doubts about it, or if you think I'm engaged in any kid play, or if you're fidgety about smelling some gun smoke except in tin-can target practice, you better quit with the ten days' advance pay I gave you while the quitting is good!"

Buck's gaze had turned to one of astonishment. Now his face flushed angrily. "I don't feel like trailing along at five dollars a day, at your expense, on any fool errand if that's what you're getting at," he retorted. "The way you seem to be going at it, if the Crow was around here, you'd probably blunder into him and get us both shot up before we had a chance to do anything about it." He finished in a tone of contempt.

"That's the difference in viewpoint," said Davitt coldly. "If we should blunder into this bandit, I'd know what to do. I've tracked down outlaws before. Just at present, I'm making it my business. I don't merely pick one out and start on his trail, either. People hire me to go after 'em. In this case, it was Sylvester Graham who sent for me. How do you suppose I arranged that confab with the sheriff last night … just by asking for it? Listen, fellow, Graham got me up here, and last night he decided I wasn't good enough to catch the Crow. So I'm going to get him on my own. I'm doing you a favor by letting you in, and if you're not the man I picked you to be, it's a good thing I found it out before you got a chance to go cold on me."

Buck's stare of wonderment changed to a flash of anger. "That's man's talk, but if you're what you claim to be, you could have said so in the first place and I'd have known what …"

"I don't take any chances by talking ahead of time," Davitt interrupted sharply. "Graham, the sheriff, your boss, Payne, and some stockmen, including young Wessel's father, and even Virginia Graham know who I am. It won't do any hurt now for you to know. But it might not have been wise last night, for there was a man in town I wanted to have see something, and that was your preparations for this trip."

"Who was the man?" asked Buck.

"A partner of the man who's traveling with the Crow," Davitt replied. "You don't think that outlaw just wanted a small bit from that bank, do you? They think he travels alone, but I know different. I ran across the trail of two men who met him up this way somewhere before I started."

"And what's the sheriff for? Why all this fuss about posses and rewards if Graham thought you could get the Crow so easy?"

"You don't think the sheriff is going to quit because I'm here, do you? Rewards have to be offered in these cases, and if no reward had been offered, it would have put the Crow on his guard. Even if that spy he had down in town knew who I was, it wouldn't do this Crow any good. He's heard of me as a man hunter and he won't think of me for a split second as being able to outthink him. Just the same, his scheme is as plain as the sky above to me."

"He'd be pleased to hear that," observed Buck sarcastically.

"No, he wouldn't," Davitt said with an edge to his words. "He'd be mad enough to shoot on sight. When it comes to scheming, the Crow is vain. Outguess him and you've got him. I've done the first."

Buck had ceased smiling. He put a hand inside his shirt and drew out a wallet. He extracted fifty dollars and tossed the wadded bills across to Davitt. "If you can show me, I'm with you," he said earnestly, "and the five dollars a day is just what you say … bird seed."

Davitt took the bills and put them in a pocket. He rolled and lighted a cigarette, looking about the wide ravine as he did so.

"The sheriff came back from his posse hunt down this way a week ago come tomorrow," he said, as if rehearsing the speech. "He found that piece of paper left by the Crow. The drawing of the black bird is the Crow's signature. It wasn't there when the sheriff took his men into the hills, so the bandit must have circled around or watched him when he came in. So the sheriff scribbled that about posting his answer in a week in hopes the Crow would see it. Get that, Buck?"

"Yeah. Did he tell you that?"

"He told me that and told me about his meeting with Graham, your boss, and two other cattlemen when he got back. Then is when Graham sent for me. He was sore because the sheriff hadn't caught the outlaw. He sent through a relative of his I had done some work for south of here. I started up here three days ago." He then told Buck briefly of his visit with Graham and the sheriff the night before.

"And you think Graham got mad because you danced with Virginia?" asked Buck with a frown.

"Not at all," replied Davitt with a smile. "He as much as told me I was too much of a kid. He thought I should have looked different. He expected somebody heavy with guns and hard looks, and he finds me dancing. Then, when he learned that I required an advance payment, it broke him down completely. He thought I was trying to make him for a thousand. The point is, Buck, that Sylvester Graham doesn't think I'm capable of coping with the Crow."

"You don't act much like a man hunter," Buck acknowledged.

"And that's a mighty good disguise, Buck," said Davitt. "I'm not old and I'm not going to let the business I'm in make me old. You know why I wanted to dance with Virginia Graham last night? Just because she is pretty? Not on your life. I was curious when I heard who she was from you. I was more curious when I saw what a stunning looker she is. But I was most curious of all to learn if she has brains. I believe she has 'em. There my interest ends, at present, although I'd like to test her out. Now if you'll pay attention, I'll tell you what I believe is the Crow's scheme, and why."

"I'm listening," Buck prompted. The cowpuncher was probably more interested than he ever had been in his life. For what Davitt had told him, and his way of telling it, coupled with the striking personality of the man, his quiet confidence, and the suggestion of a dangerous side to him, had convinced Buck that here was no ordinary Cattlemen's Association agent, or the like.

"It's a pretty safe bet to say that the Crow waited around to be sure the sheriff saw that notice he left on the tree," said Davitt. "I learned a lot about the Crow down Miles City way and in Wyoming. He doesn't know what fear is, he sneers at danger, he's sure death with his gun, and he doesn't discriminate much in selecting targets. But above everything else, he's vain. He likes to be spectacular. What's more, he would rather take a long chance to be spectacular and have it talked about, than to grab a made-to-order cinch and merely get the loot." He pinched the light from his cigarette end and flipped it away.

"When he left the Milton bank, he knew he didn't have as much money as was in that vault," Davitt continued. "Graham just made a guess at it when he said twenty thousand. It was closer to ten, as the sheriff hinted. The Crow has had enough experience to have known he wasn't getting so much. He wasn't thinking of the money as much as he was thinking of the names old Graham called him. I still think that Graham didn't know just how bad the Crow is, when he called him a blackguard, a thief, and a murderer. No one ever called the Crow even one of those names before to his face. The Crow wouldn't forget it. And he wouldn't get much satisfaction just shooting Graham down. No, sir, Graham would have to be told just what kind of a mistake he made and told at length. Therefore, the Crow would have to meet him again. Now, I see by your eyes you're beginning to see the direction my words are pointing."

"You mean he's coming back!" Buck ejaculated.

Davitt nodded with a cold smile. "Knowing the man's character as well as I do, it's as simple as telling time with a good watch," he said. "The Crow stuck around and made sure the sheriff glimpsed his notice. He probably was watching from a hiding place at the time. He saw what the sheriff scribbled on the notice, too. This isn't a hunch, it's pure reasoning. And he'd hang around for a week to read the answer. One of the sheriff's men hung up that Reward poster last night. And I saw a crony of the Crow's on the trail up here, which is one reason I wanted to ride into town with somebody who lived around here … to avoid suspicion. I picked on you."

"Did you see the Crow's man in town?" asked Buck.

"When we came out of the hotel." Davitt smiled. "And I went straight to the dance with you for as sweet an alibi as a man ever had."

Buck looked at him with open admiration. "Not bad," he conceded.

"By this time the Crow knows about the sheriff's Reward poster down there by the tree"—Davitt nodded—"he may know, too, that we rode out of town with a pack outfit, and if he does, he thinks we're deputies. He's so used to outguessing people that he thinks he's outguessing the sheriff. He figures the sheriff expected him to see that promise he scribbled on the notice and that the sheriff will have a bunch of men cached around down there to nip him when he comes back to see the answer. Will he go down to read the answer, Buck?"

"He will not," Buck blurted confidently. "He'll swing around into town for another crack at the bank while the sheriff is up here waiting."

Davitt beamed. "If I hadn't known you had some brains tucked behind your banter, I'd have left you in town, Buck. That's just what the Crow figures to do. And the week is up tomorrow. I think it's safe for us to figure on something tonight, or tomorrow night at the very latest. And knowing this country as you do, it's up to you to pick the softest spot from which the Crow can strike at the town."

"That'll be Mink Coulee," said Buck instantly. Then his eyes were shaded with a new doubt. "Listen, Davitt, if you was so sure of all this, why didn't you just wait in town for the Crow to show up?"

Davitt smiled again. "That would be just what the Crow would expect me to do … if he thought I had a notion as to his scheme and if he knew I was on his trail," he said. "I spotted his two men in the Teton brakes. One rode west to these hills, the other rode to town. If the Crow did have a suspicion someone had been called in on the hunt, he's tickled to death to hear we've taken to the hills the same as the sheriff. And you can lay to it that he'll have one of his men in town, maybe both of 'em, before he shows up himself. The man who took to the hills, Buck, knows this country, too. For all I know, the Crow was down in the brakes with them before he rode up to rob the bank. He probably told 'em to wait a couple days and then split up and do as told. He might not have been able to hold up the bank that first afternoon, you know. He probably has the man who knows the country with him. And this is going to be a night job, remember that."

"You think he's going to blow open the safe?" asked Buck.

"He could if he had to, but that's pretty rough work, Buck … and noisy. He's afraid of that new-fangled burglar alarm, too, and he wants to tell Sylvester Graham just how big a mistake he made in calling him those impolite names. Suppose he could get Graham into the bank with him and tell him just what he thought of him while he compelled him to open the vault? That's a strong vault. The Crow and his aides haven't been up against such a strong one. It would be easier the way I've suggested … it would be more spectacular … and the Crow might not kill Graham at all but leave him tied in his chair with a note on the desk with the drawing in ink of the black bird which is the Crow's signature."

"It's magic!" Buck exclaimed. "By the way you've figured it out, it sounds so reasonable you might be reading that outlaw's mind. He'll make old Graham open that vault at the pistol point while his two men keep watch outside. I bet he tries it tonight. He will, if the sheriff leaves town."

"The sheriff is going to carry out his plan," drawled Davitt. "Crow meat, he called our man. That cinched it. And look, here comes a visitor up the trail. Let's tidy the things up before the gent gets a line on us."

CHAPTER SEVEN

The newcomer walked his horse up the ravine from the main trail, looking about at the meadow and slopes, evidently intent upon giving the impression that he had chanced that way. He was quite close to Davitt and Buck before he gave them his curious attention. He raised a hand in negligible salute as he checked his horse. He had a round, expressionless face, mild blue eyes, a large nose, and wore a stubble of reddish beard. Buck managed to shake his head slightly at Davitt to convey the information that he didn't know the man.

"Fishing for trout?" inquired the stranger in a choppy voice.

"For a meal, you mean," Buck corrected. "We just ate it."

"I see." The rider, who made no move to dismount, nodded sagely. "Reckon you boys are cowhands like myself. I'm Riley, from out east of Benton. I saw you boys in here and rode in to make sure of my directions. Going camping?"

"Don't know any Rileys from out Benton way," said Buck, ignoring the question. "That's off our range. We're from the Payne Ranch. What direction you want to make sure of?"

"I'm heading up the north fork of the Teton, ain't I?"

"You are, if you keep on the trail you turned off of," replied Buck. "Up this way, you're heading for some tough hill travel."

"Oh, I'm going up the trail," said Riley, looking closely at the two of them. "Wouldn't be surprised if you boys was taking time off for the same reason as myself."

"What would that be?" Davitt inquired, flashing a look to Buck which indicated that he wanted to take charge of the conversation.

"I'm hoping to run across the Crow," Riley answered.

"Why, that's what ..." Davitt seemingly checked his words in confusion, and scowled. "Funny the news about that fellow would get clear over Benton way so quick," he supplemented.

"I heard it from the sheriff," Riley volunteered, his eyes betraying his keen interest. "The law passes the word around quick. That's a big reward they're offering."

"They won't have to pay it, so they're safe in offering it," Davitt said, and frowned. "The only way anybody'll catch the Crow is by finding him sound asleep." He laughed shortly. "They could have offered twice as much and have been just as safe. You figure on getting this outlaw party with the bird name?"

"I might run across him," Riley said with a shrug. "I reckon I'm not the only man in these hills with the idea in his head."

"You'll be better off just to call it an idea and let it go at that," said Davitt. "From what we've heard, this Crow isn't the right kind of person to run across. What do you know about him?"

"Just an outlaw," replied Riley. "We've had lots of 'em out our way. They get a lucky break and make a haul and then slip up somehow and get took in. If you boys run across him, you'll have a pretty good chance because there's two of you."

"Now that you've got all this off your chest, just what did you bust in on us for?" demanded Davitt coldly. "If you wanted to be put right as to the trail, you've got the information. If you

want to know anything about us, we're going fishing. You don't
look so much like a cowhand to me ... what are you ... a deputy
sheriff?"

Riley indulged in a guffaw. "That's not bad," he said, grinning. "If I look like one of them, I won't have much chance if ..."

"Seems to me like you've got too many ifs handy," Davitt said
sharply. "Whoever you are, we're minding our own business and
we expect strangers to do the same."

"Oh, I can take a hint," said Riley with a scowl. "Thanks." He
turned his horse. "I don't think you're cowhands, either," he flung
over his shoulder. "If you were, you'd be more sociable." With this
he trotted back the way he had come.

Buck looked at Davitt to see him smiling grimly. "You hit
it on the head, he said. "That hombre is no more cowhand than
you are."

"If I'm not mistaken that fellow is one of the Crow's men,"
said Davitt thoughtfully. "You're sure you never saw him before?"

"I know most everybody on this range that's been here a
while," said Buck. "Maybe he's a new hand, or maybe he's from
Benton, but he don't act like cow people to me."

"Nor to me!" Davitt ejaculated. "And you'll notice he was
careful to look us over. He isn't just riding around looking everybody over. We've got to get packed and get started so he can see
that we're on our way. That's likely what he wants to see, so we'll
oblige him."

"I was afraid you might decide to take him in tow," said
Buck.

"Grab him, you mean?" Davitt put the question with a smile.

"And that would have been bad." Buck nodded. "It would
have put this Crow wise to us for sure and certain."

Davitt's gaze was cool and calculating. "Looks like we make a
good team, Buck," he said. "Your brains work good when they get

stirred up. That fellow won't bother anybody he thinks is working for the sheriff, either. Bring up the horses and we'll throw on this pack and slope."

* * * * *

They rode down the ravine to the main trail and again turned up into the higher hills. It was now well past noon and Buck had selected their camping place for the night. Davitt had stipulated that it be at a point from which they could see the lower hills and where their fire could be seen for a long distance. Buck had asked no questions and had picked his location according to instructions. He was learning about man hunting from a master, and discovering it was an art.

They made slow progress, partly because they did not wish to go very far before making camp, and partly—in which their plans were aided—by the fractiousness of the pack horse. The animal did not take kindly to the work and frequently bolted or balked. Twice they had to take off the pack and rearrange it, making it fast with a double-diamond hitch. They worked slowly and finally made camp in the late afternoon after having traveled but ten or twelve miles since their meal before noon. The frequent delays had enabled them to rest their horses, and when they stopped for the day, it was only the pack animal that was tired.

Davitt spoke little while they went about the work of putting up the pup tent, cutting a few small firs and making a bough bed, and attending to other details which would have convinced anyone who might have been watching unseen that they were indeed on a pleasure expedition into the mountains. From the shelf of meadowland on the slope that Buck had selected they had a good view of the hills below and the prairie beyond. Buck pointed down to where the North Fork flowed out of the foothills and then to a bit of rough land which reached out into the prairie about two miles north of the stream.

"Mink Coulee is about five miles out from that snarl on the prairie," he said. "I know a shortcut from here that'll take us down there quicker than we could make it by the trail we come up and we'd be pretty sure of not meeting up with anybody."

"That's the ticket," Davitt said. "Now we'll get supper, and we'll let 'em see some smoke and later we'll let 'em see some fire in case the Crow and his partners should look up this way. You can lay to it that the sheriff's men won't be making any such show. If our visitor was what I had him pegged for, the Crow will be more interested in us than in any posse. I still think he's traveling with the outlaw. But I'm worried just the same."

"So am I," Buck said unexpectedly, with a frown.

"Why so?" asked Davitt curiously, eyeing Buck closely.

"It's all too doggoned simple!" Buck exploded.

Davitt's eyes lighted with genuine pleasure. "You said something," he agreed. "We've got this thing figured out too smooth. I've been puzzling my brain all the way up here and can't find a flaw in our reasoning. That's why I'm suspicious. There's bound to be complications, or this job will be different from any I ever worked on. It just isn't in the pictures for it to work out clocklike, but I can't make out where the hitch is … unless we were wrong from the beginning. And this man who calls himself Riley … well, his happening along seems to show we are on the right track."

"It just wouldn't be natural," argued Buck. "Everything coming out so perfect, I mean. I guess I'm simple to listen to a fairy story and believe it. I could make the same thing up in my head … why, say." He looked startled. "I've heard of hold-ups being pulled and such, and I've sat down and figured out what I would do if I had pulled the trick, and sometimes that's just what the ornery cuss did."

"Why not?" Davitt asked blandly. "Put yourself in the other

fellow's place. There's a lot in it. But in this case, we've got pretty good grounds to believe we know the Crow's plans. He rode west, but he didn't keep on going west. Instead, he's got two men with him and I've seen one of them in town, and maybe we both saw the other here. No, we're all right in our deductions ... I think that's what they call them. And Riley spoke the truth, whether he intended to do so or not, when he said an outlaw always makes a slip. Still, the Crow has been in the game for twenty years and, so far as I know, he's never spent a day in jail. If he ever got in jail, he'd hang. So it's safe to say he'd die rather than be taken. You couldn't stop the Crow by just covering him with a gun. He'd draw anyway!"

"Well, he won't draw on me!" Buck exclaimed, his gun whipping out of his holster with such speed that Davitt was startled.

"Why, you're a long way from being slow with your gun, Buck," Davitt drawled. "I didn't know they got that fast, just in range work."

"I practice," Buck growled, putting back his weapon.

"Handy thing, a fast draw," Davitt observed, "and just as dangerous. I suppose you can shoot straight in the bargain."

"Straight enough," was the answer. "If it comes to guns ..."

"If it comes to guns," Davitt interrupted sternly, "let me take the lead ... if there's time. If it slants that way when you're alone, be sure and be certain, both as to cause and aim. A miss as to cause, Buck, is a whole lot worse than a miss as to aim. There's more to that than it sounds, just hearing me say it."

Buck looked him in the eyes and whatever he saw there satisfied him. "Let's get supper," he said. "The sun's going down and we'll want to start when dusk comes."

* * * * *

While they ate and during the hour after sunset, when the soft, rosy haze drifted over the green hills and the golden billows of plain, Davitt talked on with Buck, and Buck mostly listened. Davitt told him of adventures he had had in the years after he had broken away from straight ranch work. He dwelt on activities as an Association agent in tracking down rustlers, breaking up bands of horse thieves, and of a few experiences in capturing robbers and bolder outlaws. He passed lightly, and distastefully, over a killing or two, and explained at length how he had once let a youthful offender go free and had covered up his trail. These adventures had been packed into the short space of five years, and of the time before that he told practically nothing.

"It's a lonesome job," he said, with a wistful note in his voice, "and I mix in a good time whenever I have a chance. The prized possession that saves me is a sense of humor." He looked at Buck and grinned at him, and from that moment Buck knew he liked him.

As the twilight fell and dusk deepened in the high hills, Davitt kept the fire burning. "We'll let 'em see that spark of red till it's almost dark," he told Buck. "Then we'll put it out before we leave. But those that have seen it won't forget it, and the impression that it is here will burn on long into the night. That's what I call a ghost fire. It's fed by the flames of imagination. They'll think we're still here."

"When you said there was something in an outlaw always being liable to make a slip, did you mean you think the Crow will slip?" Buck asked.

"Not in performance, but in mental alertness," Davitt said, smiling. "There's a chance that he may be so wrapped up in his desire for revenge on Sylvester Graham for the names he was called, and in the big haul he might make, that he'll overlook something ... us, for instance."

"He won't overlook you, if he knows you," Buck said grimly. "As for me, I'm only a poor cowpuncher … spare me!" He chuckled.

"Let's get going," said Davitt suddenly, scooping a handful of fresh earth from the pile he had turned, and throwing it on the fire.

CHAPTER EIGHT

The night was two hours old when Davitt and Buck emerged from the last clump of trees dividing the foothills from the flowing plain, alive with shadows under the dancing stars. They drew rein on a knoll at the extremity of the rough finger that reached out into the prairie, two miles north of the stream which marked the trail by which they had entered the hills, and five miles west of Mink Coulee.

As they looked out over the vast domain, Buck straightened in his saddle. "There!" he exclaimed breathlessly. "See it? A racing shadow! A rider streaking from the hills toward Mink. It's probably that fellow who rode in on us this morning."

Davitt had descried the fleet, bobbing blot of shadow before Buck had ceased speaking. He nodded. "The messenger with the word that everything is in order," he said in a satisfied tone. "You picked the right spot, Buck. The Crow is more than likely going to strike with a hard ride from the coulee to town. I can't figure why any other rider would be speeding across the prairie at such a rate."

"Sure I'm right," said Buck in some excitement. "Listen,

Mel,"—he used Davitt's first name quite naturally for the first time—"we've got a piece of riding of our own to do. That fellow's out of sight almost right now and he can't see us. He didn't have time to spot us on the trail and get out that far from the hills ahead of us. He was waiting till he was sure no one had left the hills and it was dark enough for him to cut loose across the open. He's got rolling country to the coulee. We'll cut down southeast and beat it toward town and take a chance on spotting 'em when they come in. We can ride our horses for all they're worth because we won't have to chase out of town afterward, while they'll have to save theirs going in. Let's get going."

He glanced quickly at Davitt, who flashed a smile, and they were off. If the cowpuncher could have read Davitt's thoughts, he would have felt complimented, for Davitt was pleased with Buck's enthusiasm, his quickness in spotting the lone rider, and his immediate decision as to their plan of action. Buck was no ordinary cowpuncher in Davitt's mind.

For going on an hour, they swung at a fast pace around the southern boundary of the rolling prairie land in which was the deep gash known as Mink Coulee. Then they came to a few cottonwoods, alders, and willows which grew about a spring between the coulee and town. At Buck's word of warning they approached this spot, cautiously prepared for a possible blaze of guns. But it would have been impossible for riders to cover the distance between the coulee and the spring without being seen by Buck and Davitt and they reached the shadows of the trees without sign of hostility or ambush.

"Now we're ahead of 'em," Buck told Davitt. "We can streak for town with these trees between us and the coulee and get far enough out so they couldn't spot us even from here. There's the chance that that rider cut straight through and met up with the Crow here, but …"

"We'll assume that he didn't," Davitt broke in. "The Crow would hardly wait in this comparatively open spot, for he would have had to have been here before dark if he was to wait for his messenger here. He would have had to get here while he knew no one was here, I mean. We've gone this far on headwork, now we'll have to go on close to town where you can wait for sign of 'em while I go in."

"You going ahead?" asked Buck, surprised.

"To make sure the Crow isn't there already, for one thing," replied Davitt, "and to be near Graham's house, for another. You'll have to bring the word, Buck. And I'm not sure we've got the Crow's movements down pat. I'm still looking for complications. It dreams too easy. Maybe we're just riding to get the night air."

"No, we're not," said Buck in a hoarse whisper. "Here they come."

Davitt had to strain his eyes to catch sight of the rapidly moving dots in the direction of the coulee. Without a word he shook out his reins and Buck followed him as he galloped around the trees and straightened out for the race to town.

Buck caught sight of his companion's eyes in the starlight and was struck by the look in them. Davitt's gaze was a brilliant steel-blue flame, the cowpuncher thought; the cold, piercing scrutiny of the man hunter racing to the kill. Davitt seemed transformed into another person entirely, and Buck sensed at once that here was a match for any outlaw. The next moves would call for quick thinking, cool nerves, lightning action. And Buck shivered with the thrill of it.

They pushed their mounts at racing speed across the shadowy plain. Buck felt like crying out with admiration as he watched Davitt's horse perform. Davitt had to hold the animal, or he would have left Buck behind, even though Buck was riding one of the best horses ever bred on the Payne Ranch. But Buck felt no great chagrin. It was to be expected, he reflected, that a man like Davitt, whose life at times had depended on his mount, would have a superb horse. It seemed as though they literally ticked off the miles as they sped toward the slowly forming blot upon the plain that was Milton.

They came upon cattle as they neared the town and circled the herd, knowing that the riders behind would have to follow their example or be seen if cowpunchers were standing guard. When clear of the cattle, they straightened out again and a last spurt brought them to the trees along the stream that flowed through Milton. Here Davitt reined in his horse and they stopped.

"How many riders did you make out back there, Buck?" Davitt asked.

"I was thinking there were two, but we didn't take any too long a look," replied the cowpuncher.

"I figured two myself," said Davitt. "That would account for the Crow and the spy we think we saw in the hills. There should be a man in town. We'll leave our horses in the trees and go in afoot. If there is a man in town, we'll have to watch out that he doesn't see us, for the Crow is smart enough to make sure that he's all right before he starts operations."

"Sure." Buck nodded. "He'll post his two men outside the bank."

"Now, listen," said Davitt, keeping his tone low. "This man here may have been watching for two riders. If he was, he'll probably think we are the men he was looking for …"

"Not a chance," Buck put in. "The Crow makes a small figure in the saddle and we're tall men."

"But did you notice the way I rode the last distance?" Davitt smiled. "I hugged my horse's neck till it would take an expert in broad daylight to tell how tall I was. People are easy fooled in this light. Chances are, if someone was watching, he'll give some kind of a signal. But the Crow is too crafty to take his horses right into the street to attract attention. He wants time to do this job. If you could move their horses … no! You've got to watch the outside of the bank, too." Davitt frowned in thought.

"I propose to be right in there at headquarters," Buck said stoutly. "Three is too many for you to tackle alone, in the first place, and I'm in on the play all the way through for the second and last place. If anybody had been going to signal, they would have done it by now."

"All right," said Davitt slowly. "Buck, I'm going to let my personal feelings have their run in this. I'm going to get into the bank with the Crow and Graham, if the Crow works that way, and if he tries it the other way, we'll just naturally have to shoot 'em down in the act. You hide out near the bank. I'm going to Graham's house. I still believe I figured it out right."

It was shortly afterward that Davitt stole noiselessly under the trees and among the shrubs of Sylvester Graham's front lawn. There still were lights in the house although it was midnight. Davitt crept to a window and looked into the front room. He saw the banker in a deep arm chair by the table, reading. No one else was in the room. The next moment Davitt nearly cried out in astonishment at what he saw. The Crow had stepped lightly into the room from the hall!

Davitt drew back from the window instantly, having caught one good look at the narrowed, cruel eyes of the outlaw, and the gun in his hand. The thought flashed through Davitt's mind that the bandit had come to town ahead of his two men; that he had set the hour of midnight for his infamous work and had depended on his men to warn him if all was not well before that time; that one of the men had been in town and had ridden to Mink Coulee to tell of the departure of the sheriff and had waited there for the other accomplice while the Crow came in.

"Don't make a sound." The hissing of the Crow's voice barely reached Davitt's ear. "Get up and come with me, or I'll put a slug in your heart. Squawk or come." The threat from the outlaw's tongue seemed to vibrate on the still air.

Davitt drew his weapon and peered stealthily inside. There was no time for a fleeting doubt as to the wisdom of his decision to get the Crow in Graham's presence. One reason for his being there was that he was afraid the banker might refuse to obey the bandit's orders. Davitt now could shoot the Crow down without warning and be justified. But some innate sense of fair play, warped and out of place in this instance, held him back. In another few moments Graham had risen and was between Davitt and the outlaw. The Crow backed out the door, his gun almost touching the banker's chest, as Graham walked with him, his hands in the air. They disappeared, and the scuffle of hurried feet came to Davitt's ears. It had happened so quickly and smoothly that Davitt was almost incredulous and caught himself looking at the empty arm chair and the paper on the floor.

Then Davitt dashed around the end of the porch. But the outlaw and his prey were not in sight. They had left by another way? Davitt ran lightly up the steps and opened the screen door. As he entered the hall, Virginia Graham, a lovely vision in a white negligee, appeared at its farther end. For a space Davitt stood, stunned by the girl's beauty.

"Why, Mister Davitt!" Virginia exclaimed in surprise.

"Did anyone pass out that way?" Davitt asked quickly.

"No. Father is in the living room, if you wish to see him."

He reached her in three long, rapid strides. "The Crow was just here," he told her in a tense voice. "He took your father out at the point of his gun. Which way could they have gone to get to the bank quickly? Tell me, for I don't know these locations. Show me the shortcut to the bank."

"Don't be absurd," said the girl, her eyes glowing suspiciously. "Father!" she called loudly.

Davitt seized her by her shoulders and shook her. "I tell you the Crow caught your father alone in front and made him go out with him," he said fiercely. "I happen to know that outlaw is taking him to the bank to make him open the safe. Which way have they gone?"

"Impossible," cried the girl angrily. "Father said you were a crazy …"

"Virginia, tell me how your father gets to the bank quick when he's in a hurry," Davitt commanded sternly. "If you don't, I'll have to run around by way of the main street and I may get there too late. It's an even chance this minute that your dad doesn't get back alive."

The deadly seriousness of his tone and the look in his eyes convinced her just as he flung her away from him with a snort of disgust and started for the front door. She caught him before he could leave.

"This way." She turned him into a room opposite the living room—a small parlor—and pointed to partly opened French windows. He hurried through them and found himself on a small side porch with the star-filled sky showing through a lane in the trees.

"Through the grounds to a street, one block from the bank …"

Davitt waited for no more but leaped down the few steps and ran through the trees. He came to the street and turned in the direction of the center intersection. No one was in sight. He crept along the shadows until he could see the rear of the bank. A faint light showed in a window which he surmised was that of Graham's private office. Surely the Crow's companions hadn't reached the bank. And this time Davitt felt he had an assistant upon whom he could depend. He crossed the street, slipped to the rear door of the bank, and found it unlocked. He opened the door noiselessly and let himself in. He could hear the low tone of the Crow's sinister voice in the private office.

"You called me names, you penny-pinching, fat-faced toad," the Crow was purring, "and now I've come to collect for them. It'll hurt you more to pay in cash and get a slap and a laugh for a receipt than for me to kill you. But you must be careful, toad, or you'll pay two ways." The outlaw's evil laugh shivered in the room.

CHAPTER NINE

Buck had reckoned closely on his time and had not followed Davitt's instructions, brief and hurried as they had been, to the letter. While Davitt was making his way to the Graham house, having secured directions from Buck, the latter had made a swift reconnaissance in the vicinity of the bank and had hurried back to where he could glimpse the riders when they entered town. For Buck had decided that instead of keeping an eye on the bank, it would be wiser, and more productive of results to watch the Crow. He could not know that the Crow already was in town. When trouble started, the Crow was bound to be in the center of it.

Thus, Buck succeeded in catching sight of the two riders before they gained the shelter of the trees along the stream at the edge of town. A smothered exclamation escaped his lips as he noted that the two horsemen were of much larger build than was attributed to the Crow. As he saw them come galloping in, he became convinced that neither of them was the notorious outlaw.

With this conviction he hurried back through the darkened street toward the bank. Suddenly a lithe figure darted from the trees around the corner and started across the street. As Buck was near the corner, and about to cross, the two men nearly collided. Buck caught the glint of starlight on dull metal and leaped aside, whipping out his own gun.

"Oh, it's you!" exclaimed a voice, which Buck recognized instantly as belonging to Chester Wessel. "Where you been all day, Buck? Back to the ranch? Come here a minute."

Buck quickly followed Wessel into the deeper shadows. The youth appeared greatly excited and Buck was at once keenly alert with more than mere curiosity. "Take it easy," he warned. "What's the idea of the gun, Chet?"

Wessel grasped him by the arm and his words came swiftly in a low, hoarse tone. "You know that fellow Davitt who was here last night? Virginia told me about him and I got more out of Old Man Payne. He's a fake, Graham thinks. Said he was here to catch the Crow, but he's probably in with him. He's been hiding all day and when I left the Graham house a while ago, I saw him sneaking through the trees. If he was going there for any decent purpose, he wouldn't be sneaking, would he? I watched and later I saw two shadows slip out the side door and I think he's taking Graham to the bank."

"Well, what of it?" Buck demanded. "Is that any reason why you should chase around with a gun in your hand?"

"Robbery, you fool!" Wessel blurted. "I thought I caught sight of another man up there … a shorter, slight man. It might even be the Crow." The youth pinched Buck's arm as if to convince him. He had taken the accidental meeting with Buck as a matter of course, which was not strange since he had known him for years and could not be expected to be suspicious.

Buck was startled. A light dawned upon him. The two men who had ridden into town were the Crow's look-outs and the outlaw had been in town all the time!

"Come on," urged Wessel, pulling at his arm.

Buck yanked him back. "Calm down a little till your brains cool off," he said. "You're flying off at the handle and dreaming things at the same time. What're you talking about robbery and what do you figure on doing?" It was dangerous to have Wessel butting in in this way and Buck realized he would have to restrain him and look after his own affairs, and Davitt's, at the same time.

"He's taking Graham to the bank, I tell you!" cried Wessel in great excitement. "It's attempted robbery and I'm going to give it to him on sight."

Buck caught the youth as he was lunging to break away. He threw his left arm about Wessel's neck and shut off his speech with his left hand pressed tightly over his mouth. Then, with his right hand, he jerked the gun from Wessel's grasp. But Wessel swung his left enough to knock the weapon from Buck's grasp.

This was not time for parley. Buck threw Wessel from him and drove his right to the jaw, knocking him on the grass. As he bent to pick up the gun, Buck glimpsed two shadowy figures run across the street at the intersection. The Crow's two companions. They disappeared at once in the darkness under the trees.

Davitt's warning to watch the bank seemed to roar in Buck's ears. He started to run to the corner, and then, remembering Wessel, he turned back, but the short interval of precious time had enabled Wessel to recover his faculties and he leaped for his gun, grabbed it, and dashed through the trees before Buck could reach him.

Buck swore and started on a dead run for the bank.

* * * * *

Mel Davitt stood in the narrow, dim corridor in the rear of the bank, gun in hand, his lips pressed tightly, and listened to the Crow.

"You ain't got so much to say this time, eh, Graham?" sneered the outlaw. "They call me the Crow and I call you the Toad. Do you know why? Because a crow is smarter than a toad. It ain't smart to call names, Toad. I could call you a fool, but I don't have to because you know you're a fool already. You were a fool to talk mean to me. You're fool enough this minute to be thinkin' you'd like to take a chance with me and yell or something. Go open the vault, Toad, and we'll carry the plunder out in your own sacks. Listen!"

A tapping on the front window was plainly heard.

"My men!" cried the bandit in triumph. "On time to the second and the coast is clear. I'd already caught the signal when you pricked your ears at the mockingbird's warble. Crows and mockingbirds and toads. Step out and open that vault, Graham, or I'll drill you where you stand."

Davitt tensed for his spring into the room as he heard Graham walk to the vault. Hidden batteries responded the next instant and from the front of the bank on the street came the harsh, resonant, clanging of a gong, shattering the stillness of the night into ringing atoms of sound that awoke the town.

Davitt literally hurled himself through the open doorway into the office as a shot rang out. A gun blazed in his face and he crashed into the huge desk and sprawled over it, knocking the lamp to the floor. In a moment he dropped to the side of the desk, firing over it. Shots rang out behind the bank and Davitt threw himself out into the corridor in time to see the slight form of the outlaw spring from the open door.

In that fleeting moment Davitt saw two faces, ghostlike in the dim light of the stars. Chet Wessel and Buck were there! A snaky tongue of fire licked at the blackness under the trees and Buck whirled, his gun flaming in the direction from which the shot had come. There were no more fiery tongues from that quarter.

But Wessel seemed in the Crow's path as the outlaw darted for the side street. Davitt sent a futile bullet toward the twisting, leaping form, and bounded in pursuit. Buck was firing again—past Davitt. Then Wessel went to the ground, his gun blazing as he cried out from the bullet to his leg.

A vision of white, wraith-like, seemed to drift across before Davitt's eyes and a little choking cry came from the rear of the bank.

Then Davitt's voice rang clear above the clamor of the gong, the shouts of aroused citizens, the distant pound of flying hoofs:

"Stop, Renwick! Take it coming like a man, and not going like a crow!"

The outlaw spun about in the middle of the street. His figure looked grotesque and misshapen, but the darting fire in his eyes was the venom of rage and hatred, contempt for law or life—the defiance of the killer!

"A toad and now a rat!" he shrilled between his teeth. "Here's your ticket, Davitt."

The voice seemed still on the air when the guns roared their message to the breathless throng. Renwick, the Crow, went to his knees, raised his gun again and dropped it as Davitt walked slowly toward him. Then he swayed and fell in the dust as the crowd broke to make way for the sheriff who came riding in with a dozen men behind him.

Davitt burst into Graham's office in the bank a minute later. Another lamp had been lighted, and Graham was sitting in his chair. Virginia was there, holding a handkerchief against her father's left side, an arm about his neck. Graham was coatless, his shirt was open, he was holding something tight in his right hand.

"Are you hit ... hard?" asked Davitt, meeting the banker's cold gaze.

"It glanced off into the fleshy part of his side." It was Virginia who answered.

Graham held his right hand over the desk, opened it, and a metal spectacle case fell against the polished surface. "He made the mistake of giving me time to put up my glasses," he said calmly. "The case deflected the bullet. I suppose you …" His eyes put the question.

"Yes, I got him," Davitt said in a tone of relief. He pointed to the dented case. "I'd heard of such things, but never believed it could happen. I'll give you credit for the nerve to set off that alarm."

* * * * *

Although it was two in the morning, the lights still burned in Sylvester Graham's living room. The banker was lying comfortably on the couch with Virginia sitting beside him in a chair. The doctor had left just before the arrival of Sheriff Drew, Frank Payne, who had stayed over in town, Davitt, and Buck.

"I had it figured out the same way, almost," the sheriff was saying, frowning slightly at Davitt, who had been explaining his procedure in bringing about the end of Renwick, the outlaw known as the Crow. "I spotted that man in the hills and I started for town when I got word from a lookout north of where he came out of the hills. Meanwhile, you had got started."

"There wasn't any time to lose," said Davitt dryly.

"He fooled me by getting back into town so soon," the sheriff growled. "I reckon I figured a night too late, or ahead of time."

"He fooled me, too," Davitt said with a faint smile. "And, thanks to our banker friend here, I made what might have turned out to be the worst mistake of my career."

The others looked at him with new interest. Davitt nodded to the banker. "You made me mad, same as you angered Renwick. I expect it made him maddest, though, when I called him by his right name. I don't believe he knew I was on his trail for sure till that moment. But you said you didn't believe I was capable and that I was trying to make you for a thousand or bleed you for expenses. I decided I'd take the Crow with you looking on. He was the wink of an eye too fast for me. I'd like to have that spectacle case for a souvenir."

"Never mind what I said … just forget it," said Graham with a gesture as if to dismiss the matter. "It wasn't just luck that I didn't get hit below the case in the right spot. I heard you bust into the room and so did he … it caused him to shoot a bit wild."

"I'm not taking too much credit," said Davitt. "But I'll accept the bank's five-thousand-dollar reward you said there were no strings attached to. After all, this is a sort of business with me."

"And I'll turn over the county's reward," said the sheriff. "You've earned it and it's worth the money."

"I reckon that's coming to Buck, here," said Davitt. "He put Renwick's pals out of business and probably saved young Wessel's life by plugging him in the leg, so he'd fall before the Crow could bore him. Buck's a partner in this business, you see."

"Why didn't you tell me?" Frank Payne asked Buck, scowling.

"Well, we agents don't usually tell what we know in advance," drawled Buck, winking at Davitt, who was smiling broadly. "You see after you fired me …"

"Oh, your job's waiting for you," Payne broke in. "You'd have got it back, anyway, and you know it."

"Yes, but I'd have had to work a long, long time at it to get five thousand iron men," Buck pointed out slyly. "Now I don't see how I can afford to take it back. As soon as I can finish readin' *The Rise and Fall of the Roman Empire*, I'm going into this business regular."

He nodded as Payne and the sheriff looked puzzled, and Davitt laughed outright. "I'm making Buck a proposition," Davitt explained, sobering. He saw Buck's eyes light up and nodded to him slightly.

"Meanwhile," Davitt continued, "I'll have to thank Miss Virginia for her assistance." He raised his brows at Sylvester Graham who was staring in astonishment. "It was your daughter, Mister Graham, who showed me the shortcut to the bank after I had watched you and the Crow go out of the room. I was watching through the window. I couldn't find out which way you two had gone until Miss Virginia …"

"Had to point out the shortcut or have her arm pinched in two," the girl interrupted with a flush.

"Well, we can thrash all these details out later," said Buck in a cheerful voice. "I'm thinking you did Mel Davitt an injustice, Mister Graham. I'm only a cowpuncher, but I'm old enough to recognize a real man and a capable one when I run up against him as hard as I did Davitt. You ought to make good for what you said about him and for not trusting him."

"How much?" demanded Graham with a deep scowl.

"Now there you go," Buck complained. "Always reckoning in terms of bills or specie. You'd be doing the polite thing if you'd invite him to dinner, say. Something like that." He beamed.

Virginia Graham's laugh rippled forth. "I'm inviting the two of you," she said, giving Davitt a look that caused him to smile graciously at his new partner.

"In which case, we accept," sang Buck with a wink at Sylvester Graham.

CHAPTER TEN

"Doggone!" Buck exclaimed, looking up from a letter he held in his hand. "Who do you suppose this is from, Mel?" He stared across the small room of the hotel at Davitt who was lying on the bed.

Davitt glanced from the book he was reading to Buck at the table by the window.

"I should judge it was from someone connected with the State Bank of Milton," he drawled, "having noted the name of that bank in the upper left-hand corner of the envelope."

"It's from old Sylvester Graham himself!" Buck exploded. "He wants to see us at the bank at ten o'clock this bright summer morning, so he writes." He continued to study the letter with a frown on his bronzed features.

"Well, it's a good thing we got up and had breakfast early," Davitt said, and yawned. "We're both customers of the bank ... being depositors ... and he's president of that staunch institution, so ..."

"He knew how to run that bank before he ever saw either of us, so if you're thinking he's wanting our advice or your advice, rather, why ..."

"The letter was addressed to Davitt and Granger," Davitt interrupted. "If it hadn't been so addressed, I wouldn't have given it to you to open. Maybe he wants us to close out our accounts."

"Not a chance," said Buck scornfully. "Too much money, my friend. With me putting in the five thousand, and you the other five thousand in rewards we got for finishing the Crow's outlaw career, and you adding another five thousand you were packing to your bit, and another five thousand from Denam … him turning down twenty thousand dollars in deposits that'll give him more keys to mortgages? Not on your life! You don't know Graham. Why, when we put that money in the bank he almost gave me a respectful look when he said I was lucky." He puckered his brows in thought, then his face lightened. "I'll bet he's got a scheme to get us to invest that money in something he's got to offer. Maybe he's scared we'll lose it gambling or something."

"We might at that," Davitt said, crossing his feet, encased in polished riding boots, on the newspaper at the foot of the bed.

"What I mean is, why should he write to us in the first place, and why should he be so particular about the exact time he wants to see us," grumbled Buck. "This letter is the same as giving us our orders. I happen to know you won't be high-toned by anybody, and as long as you've taken me in as a partner in this man-hunting business, I feel the same way. We've got to be careful of our reputation."

Mel Davitt chuckled. "That's the idea, buckaroo, and don't forget that I'm the head of this firm." He laid his book aside. "A while back you said I talked too good to be a cowpuncher, and I told you I got my learning by reading books. If you'd spent more time in reading books, instead of chasing doggies with a hot branding iron that belonged to somebody else, you'd be able to fathom that letter at a glance. Every ranch I ever heard of had a Buck … but if you travel with me, it won't be long before I'll have 'em calling you by your first name … your real name, I mean."

"That'll be a great help," Buck said sarcastically. "Well, you ought to know about everything. You're a year older than me, anyway. You must be all of twenty-six, and you must have put in full time during that extra year."

"There you go," frowned Davitt. "The quickest and easiest way a man can make a fool of himself is to get mad. Too bad you never read Sherlock Holmes. That hombre thought and worked right along the same lines I do. I'll give him credit. You remember how I outguessed that bank robber, the Crow?"

"Sure," replied Buck blandly. "You outguessed him fine, except he was already in town when we thought he was out on the prairie scratching his head trying to make up his mind whether to come in or not."

"That," said Davitt airily, with a wave of his hand, "merely goes to show the contingencies with which we have to cope. Now, take that letter from Sylvester Graham, Esquire. He's the president and guiding hand of the bank here in Milton which is known as one of the strongest stockmen's banks on this north range. An inexperienced cowhand like yourself ..."

"I'm a top hand, mister," Buck broke in indignantly.

"With cows, yes." Davitt nodded. "But at present we're dealing with bankers. Graham is a big banker. I suppose you'd expect him to drop into the lobby downstairs and leave word with the clerk that he wanted to see us ... or maybe come up to the room. Perhaps you'd expect him to look us up in some joint where we were playing cards. *Humph!* The man has a station in life to maintain. Besides, he's a businessman. What does he do? Why, he writes a letter in his office and has the government of the United States deliver it to us. That's one of the things the government is for, Buck."

"Isn't it strange I never thought of that," Buck said vaguely.

"Not at all," said Davitt with gusto. "You were not supposed to think of that. You're not accustomed to getting letters in the first place. But let's go further. He wrote the letter because he wants to see us, of course. If he just wanted to see us casual like, he'd have said for us just to drop in today or tomorrow. Pinch your brains. Instead of that, he writes that he definitely wants to see us today. Now I guess you understand."

"Perfectly," said Buck dryly. "It's as clear as I-declare that he wants to see us today. He said that right in this here letter."

"But that isn't all," Davitt admonished, holding up a finger. "He wants to see us at ten o'clock this morning. Why is that?"

"Because he's got to foreclose mortgages the rest of the day, and then go to Great Falls for the rest of the week to get his mustache trimmed down so he can say 'no' sharper," replied Buck.

"You may be able to spin a rope, Buck, but humor is too subtle a commodity for you to try to handle," Davitt said severely. "Graham isn't so busy that he has to make a definite appointment unless it is absolutely necessary. In fact, we could drop into the bank and see him most any time of day. In my opinion, he wants us there at a specific hour because somebody else is going to be there then and he aims to bring us together. It's easy enough to say any old time to one man, or two, if they are together, but bringing two different parties together is another thing. Now you have it."

"Sounds sensible," Buck conceded. "Who's the other party?"

"That's what makes it interesting, and also makes it imperative that we be at the bank at ten o'clock," Davitt said, getting up.

"Maybe it's a case," said Buck, brightening.

"It's possible that Graham may be bringing us in touch with a client," said Davitt. "Do you know what a client is, Buck?"

"A client is a fellow that goes to a lawyer and gets himself made into a sap," returned Buck testily, rising from his chair. "The way you're combing your hair, you'd think old Sylvester was expecting his daughter to be present."

"That's not impossible, either," was Davitt's comment. "But Virginia doesn't have to arrange a meeting with me through her father."

"Oh, no? So you're just like that since he invited you to dinner with her," Buck scoffed.

Davitt scowled at him. "We were just the way we are now since the first time I met her and danced with her," he said sternly. "And that lets you out, wild boy."

"I'm not trying to pry into your love affairs," the cowpuncher said, grinning. "I don't have to have money to grease mine with, though, and I'm holding that you didn't put ten thousand in old Graham's bank just because you thought it would be safe there."

"That'll do for you!" snapped Davitt. "We have business on hand and it's nearly ten o'clock."

"Glad you remembered it," said Buck calmly. "Don't forget a man can make a fool of himself quick and easy over a woman just like he can by getting mad."

* * * * *

Sylvester Graham greeted them with a brief smile and a business-like good morning when they entered his private office in the bank at ten o'clock sharp in response to his curt invitation.

"I didn't know if you were still in town," he said to Davitt.

"We stayed because we didn't have anything in sight for the moment," Buck explained, lifting his brows and taking a chair.

The banker flashed a questioning glance at Davitt, saw he was smiling, then looked at Buck with disapproval. "It must be of great assistance to Davitt to have someone to speak for him," he said in a biting tone.

"I don't warm to being ignored," was Buck's sprightly retort. "Your invitation to visit you was addressed to both of us."

"That was a courtesy," Graham said with dignity. "After all, it was with Davitt that I first had business, and I'll take matters up directly with him for the present."

"What did you wish to see us about, Mister Graham?" Davitt interrupted in an easy voice as he took the chair the banker indicated.

Graham cleared his throat impressively. "Your arrival here and what followed has excited some interest," he said pompously. "An influential stockman has been experiencing some irregularity, so to speak, on his range. He thought because you were so fortunate in disposing of the desperado who robbed the bank that you might help him in his difficulty."

Davitt glanced at the clock on the wall. "He's late, isn't he?" he asked pleasantly, with a sly look at Buck.

"I arranged for him to come a few minutes after you got here," Graham informed them, frowning. "He saw you then and told you about …"

"Oh no, no," Davitt interrupted. "I merely surmised that you had arranged our visit at a time when this stockman could be here."

The banker looked at Buck doubtfully. "Anyway, I wanted a word with you beforehand. Lamby … Roy Lamby … is one of our leading stockmen, a director of this bank, and a figure in the county politics. For reasons of his own, which he will explain to you personally, he hasn't seen fit to call his trouble to the attention of the sheriff or the Cattlemen's Association."

"I see," said Davitt with a queer smile. "He wants to work on the quiet. I may as well tell you, Mister Graham, that I take no cases involving range disputes or personal grudges."

"And we're particular about how much money there is in it, too," Buck put in with a wise wink at his partner.

"Granger,"—Graham struggled to control himself and finally

his features froze sternly—"you would do better to let well enough alone," he said coldly. "Keep hold of what you stumbled onto and go back to work on Frank Payne's ranch, instead of trying to enter a game you know nothing about." His eyes flashed just once as he finished.

"Oh, Buck means all right," Davitt said soothingly. "If you have something to tell us before this man Lamby gets here, we better have it now."

"It isn't a range dispute or a grudge," said Graham, "and I would have you know that I'm interested only indirectly in the matter because, in a way, Lamby is a business associate of mine, and he is a good customer of the bank. I'm always for anything that is for the good of the range up here and I won't see Lamby or anyone else imposed upon if I can help it. I can't say that I thoroughly approve of his desiring to take this business up with you."

"In that case, we better let Lamby come to us himself of his own free will," Davitt said, coolly rising.

"No, no," Graham said quickly, shaking his head. "Sit down. I didn't tell him I disapproved and I'm not sure that I do. Somebody has been stealing his cattle. That is the case in point."

"Rustling," Davitt said, sitting down again. "It really should be reported to the association, at that. I don't know if I am free to undertake such a case unless it *is* reported."

"There, there, it's all right, I tell you," said Graham. "Of course, I want it understood that what I say is confidential." He looked quickly at Buck, apparently startled.

"Don't mind me," drawled the cowpuncher. "Mel and me are just like that when it comes to what we hear and what we tell and what we say to each other alone." He crossed two fingers and winked at the banker, who instantly drew himself up with a frown.

"Let us hope so," he rasped. "You see, Davitt, it's this way. Lamby doesn't want to get the Association stirred up because he doesn't know who the investigation might involve. He ... *ah* ... another rancher by name of Matt Hull, who has the place just north of the Triangle ... that's Lamby's ranch ... has had words with him about stock irregularities. That's about all I wish to say, but perhaps you will see the somewhat delicate position I am in. I am interested in preserving peace, that is ..."

"You want to keep on the good side of both of 'em regardless of who's stealin' the cattle," Buck suggested pleasantly.

Graham struck his desk with the palm of his right hand and glared, his lids twitching.

"There might be something in what Buck says," Davitt interposed quickly. "That would be good policy on your part, naturally. You wanted me to know about these two men in advance. Why?"

"So you would have a sense of the real situation," said the banker briskly. "You needn't mention it, but I've ... I'm expecting Hull here, too." He glanced quickly through the open doorway into the cage. "Lamby is coming now," he said in an undertone. "I'll be plain with you, Granger, and ask you as a favor to be careful what you say."

"When it comes to dealing with stockmen I'm in my home corral," Buck returned.

A minute later Graham was on his feet admitting Lamby to the office. "Davitt is here with his ... his friend," he told the rancher.

"No doubt," said Lamby in a worn, cracked voice. He was a tall, spare man, with loose, hanging mustache of sandy hue, but Davitt thought he detected humor in the pale blue eyes and felt inclined to like the man from the start. There was something about him, too, which suggested shrewdness and a nimble mind in an emergency. He must have his qualities to possess and rule one of the largest stock ranches on that great range.

"You quit the Payne outfit?" he asked Buck with a keen glance.

"I'm trailing with Davitt, here, for the present," Buck replied, looking vaguely uncomfortable. Later he was to tell Davitt that there had always been something about Lamby's look or manner that got his goat.

"I suppose Sil has told you what I wanted to see you about?" the stockman asked Davitt as he sat down, and the banker retreated behind his desk.

"He merely mentioned some stock irregularities," said Davitt.

"I told him you had lost some cattle and didn't want to take it up with the association or the sheriff," said Graham. "It was your own suggestion, you'll remember, that it might be well for you to talk to Davitt, and I arranged this meeting."

"Well, that's about the size of it," Lamby said, nodding at Davitt. "I've been losing stock and want to find out about it without stirring up the whole range. A spark, you know, can start a fire."

"In the right place," said Davitt. "If it's just a matter of details, why, we can discuss those without taking up space in Mister Graham's office. In fact, I'd rather talk about it with you, personally."

"That's all right with me," agreed Lamby. "I'm sort of in doubt whether you want to take me up in this, since it's a small matter. Then, there's the item of your pay to be considered."

"Yes, the matter of compensation should be thoroughly understood in advance," Graham said hastily, nodding his head at Lamby.

Davitt thought he discerned a quality in the stockman's look and speech that escaped the banker. "How many cattle have you lost?" he asked abruptly.

"I suppose a hundred head," replied Lamby, offhand.

"We'll take twenty-five percent of the value of stock recovered," Davitt announced without an instant's hesitation.

"Twenty-five percent!" exclaimed Graham. "Why, that's outrageous! It's ... it's absolutely preposterous!"

"Which would you prefer to lose, one hundred percent or twenty-five percent?" Davitt asked Lamby.

"Why, twenty-five percent, of course," the rancher answered.

"Then I'll make that our bit ... if I take the case," said Davitt with a sharp glance at the frowning banker. "You'll not forget the terms of this verbal agreement, Graham?"

"Why, no, of course not," Graham said, somewhat flustered. "But it's considerable. Of the two alternatives you suggest, I suppose it's the most sensible one to choose."

"Then we might as well go, Mister Lamby," Davitt said, rising. "I handle business like this in my own way, without interference, you understand? I'm holding you to the agreement as well, Mister Graham ... for I have a means of doing that."

Before the banker could speak, a series of sharp raps sounded on the door. Then the knob turned, and the door swung open before a large, florid man whose protruding eyes seemed to look at each of them at once.

"Come in, come in, Mister Hull," Graham invited in a flurried tone. "You know Lamby, of course, and this is Mel Davitt."

"I've heard of him," Hull said, closing the door and looking hard at Davitt. "Prairie detective, eh?"

"Mister Davitt, to you," said Davitt coldly.

Buck Granger chuckled and opened his eyes wide as Hull turned on him, his face dark. "And you're the gun-toting waddy I heard about, I suppose," he said harshly.

"You seem to be getting a lot of information somewhere," said Buck in an exaggerated drawl. "My name's Granger, in case you want to write it down."

"Never mind," Graham said sharply. "These men were here on business, and they were just about to leave when you came," he explained to Hull with a faint note of apology in his voice.

Hull gave no indication of hearing. He was looking at Lamby.

"I reckon you came in on that range business, Lamby. Well, if you figure on hiring this pair, you better tell 'em it isn't open season for shooting up my way."

"If I've hired 'em, it doesn't have to mean I've hired 'em to do any shooting," Lamby told him with a faint smile which curled a bit suspiciously. "You seem to be jumping at conclusions, Matt."

"You had men on my range looking for strays, so you said, and I don't like it!" thundered Hull, favoring Graham with a dark glance. "Anybody'd think somebody was stealing your cattle and that that somebody was me."

"That's not exactly fair," Lamby said quietly. "You told me you had missed some stock yourself."

"And so I have," Hull declared. "If you've hired this pair to find yours and they find mine too, I'll pay 'em as much as you do."

"And that is fair," Graham put in. "Why don't you two get together in this matter? If rustling is really going on, it's to the best interests of both of you to get to the bottom of it and stamp it out."

"That's a nice speech, but I'm willing," said Hull. "Go ahead with your scheme and I'll back you up." He looked at Graham and nodded solemnly.

"That's an excellent idea," Graham said eagerly, rubbing his hands. "There's no need to let the whole range know about it, either."

"So long as everybody's satisfied, let's trail along, Buck," drawled Davitt. "We'll be up at the Green Bottle if anybody wants to see us."

He stepped to the door with Buck close behind him. "Suppose you three plot it out so we can take hold of the plan and unravel it to suit ourselves," he said pleasantly as he opened the door.

They went out, leaving the banker and the two stockmen staring after them with incongruous expressions on their faces.

CHAPTER ELEVEN

Instead of going to the Green Bottle, Davitt led the way up the street to the hotel which they had left to keep the appointment with Sylvester Graham. Buck said nothing. He was content to let Davitt manage things in his own way and to find out for himself why this skilled prairie sleuth made his moves. He relished working with Davitt because their activities were more than likely to involve danger. But he had learned that Davitt was not altogether infallible in his shrewd deductions. He was ready to listen to a suggestion and Buck liked him all the better for this trait.

When they entered the hotel lobby, Davitt led the way through a door to the snug little bar, put up a finger at the bartender, and ordered two libations.

"Wait a minute," Buck protested in a voice that carried to his companion's ears alone. "I thought you said the rule was no drink until four o'clock in the afternoon, and then only one before supper and two in the evening."

"A very good rule," nodded Davitt with his catching smile. "An excellent rule. That is why it can be broken in an emergency, especially when it's good business. By the way, if any rules are broken when we are together, I will break them first."

"And when I'm alone, I'm to use my best judgment, I suppose," Buck grunted. "I suppose that covers the shoot first situation."

"If it is necessary to bring that particular rule into operation, Buck, never break it," said Davitt soberly. "When it comes to making a target of oneself, it is better to stick to the rule and remain alive to regret any mistake than to break the rule and become thoroughly and permanently dead. We'll play around with our drinks, for I want a little time."

There were only two other patrons in the place and Buck noticed this pair paid no attention to them. He looked at Davitt curiously and saw he was smiling to himself.

"You look pleased," he told Davitt. "What do you make of it?"

"I'm both pleased and amused," said Davitt, "and this looks as if it would turn out to be an interesting piece of work for us." He frowned thoughtfully. "Buck, I've a hunch we're being watched," he said finally. "You remember last night I kept looking past you when we were playing in that game, sitting at opposite sides of the table? Well, a little fellow was looking on, pretending he was watching the play, but I got the impression he was more interested in me than in the game."

"What did he look like?" asked Buck eagerly.

"Looked like a little bowlegged crab, with a black frowsy mustache and a pair of squinting eyes that looked as if they had been screwed into his head. If he's got a nickname it ought to be Screw-eye. We'll call him that, anyway."

"Have you seen him since, Mel?"

"That's the point," replied Davitt with another frown. "I saw him in the lobby this morning when we came down to break-fast. I'd noticed him because he's the kind of a gink a man would notice every time he saw him. Then, when we came out of the

bank just now, I saw him again. He was standing in front of the
Green Bottle. It struck me he was watching for us. He went into
that place, which is why I didn't go there. I wanted to see if he'd
drift up here. Suppose you take your drink, or spill it, and mosey
out and see if you spot anybody answering my description. If you
do, keep an eye on him, casual-like, and if you see Lamby, tell him
I'm up here."

"Suits me fine," said Buck with satisfaction. "I'll spot him
and ..." He paused and looked at Davitt thoughtfully as he tossed
off the small drink. "Maybe he was connected with that Crow
bunch we busted up and knows you from down south somewhere."

"I don't think so," Davitt said. "I know most of that crowd
and I'd never forget a pair of screw-eyes like this fellow has got.
Don't let him get wise. Remember, he probably knows you're traveling with me. Maybe he's just curious, but it pays to be careful."

When Buck Granger had gone out, the bartender approached
Davitt with a respectful mien. "You're wearing the finest hat I ever
saw," he said, jerking a thumb toward Davitt's big cream Stetson.

"Thanks," Davitt returned coolly. "I'll take it off soon."

"Oh, I didn't mean to say anything out of the way," the bar-
keeper apologized.

"I know you didn't," was Davitt's cold reply. "That's why you
wouldn't understand what I mean."

The other retreated to his nook at the lower end of the bar,
followed by Davitt's keen gaze.

At this juncture a man swung in from the hotel lobby, paused
with his legs well apart, his hands on his hips, and caught Davitt's
eye in the mirror behind the bar. He was tall, heavily built, sun-
burned, and commanding in appearance. Davitt had occasion to
look at the newcomer twice through the medium of the mirror
before the man sauntered to a place at his side.

"What do you want to see me about?" asked Davitt, without waiting for the stranger to speak and looking him directly in the eyes.

"That's a straight question, and why not? My name's Quigley. I'm Matt Hull's foreman. Maybe that'll tell you something." He nodded confidently.

"It doesn't tell me a thing except that you're working for Hull," Davitt said coldly. "What am I supposed to do, cheer?"

Quigley scowled. "You may want to cheer later on, but just now it ought to interest you, since you've taken on old Lamby's case of bellyache. You don't think I'm picking up with strangers, do you?"

"That makes it altogether different," said Davitt in a more amicable tone. "I'm to suppose that Lamby's trouble is a sort of family affair between those two ranches up there, with you as a very important figure. Well, Quigley, what's your proposition?"

Quigley signaled the bartender to cover his discomfiture. He shot an appraising look at Davitt and drew a long breath. "I guess I've got to take that as meaning well," he said slowly, "for that's the only way it'll pay you to be mean toward me."

"If that's a threat, you're wasting your time," Davitt said sharply. "And I'll tell you that any advance information you've got is wrong. If I should find out it's right, I'll make it wrong."

"Oh, you're obstinate, eh?" Quigley said with a faint sneer.

"No, but I don't like your style of opening," Davitt retorted.

"All right, I'll change it," snapped Quigley. "Lamby's told you he's been losing cattle. He's hired you and that locoed waddy to find 'em. He's got half a notion his cattle have been straying on our range and staying there. Being Hull's foreman, I don't like it. Is that plain enough?"

"That's plain enough, but, if it's true, what're you going to do about it?" Davitt asked curtly.

"I don't have to do anything about it," said Quigley angrily. "I'm just trying to meet you halfway, that's all. If there's any rustling going on up our way, I want to know about it, and I want to know who's doing it, and I want it stopped. Now I reckon you know where I stand."

Davitt pursed his lips. "Sounds straight enough. Do you happen to know anything about it?"

"If I knew anything for sure, it's a cinch I wouldn't be talking to you about it," Quigley said scornfully.

"Well, you talk as if you knew something," Davitt said, frowning. "I may like to solve riddles, but I don't like to have 'em talked at me." He looked at the other frankly.

"I can't say anything very well unless I know what you intend to do," said Quigley, leaning over his glass.

"And I can't very well tell you what I'm going to do when I don't know myself," Davitt said with a shrug. "That puts us right back where we started, except that I've learned who you are, that you've had some kind of information, that you're interested and all-fired curious, and that you've got some kind of idea in your head about this trouble up at the Triangle. That sort of gives me an edge, Quigley, and I'm content to let the matter lay as it is. There's no reason why I should talk any more with you that I can see."

"Yeah?" jeered Quigley. "Well, it's what you don't see that cuts a figure, mister. You think you've learned a lot, but you're not smart enough to keep it to yourself. If there's anything underhanded going on, it's clues you want, not just a few conclusions like you've jumped at."

Davitt's manner changed instantly. He took his drink, drew tobacco and papers from a pocket, and began to roll a cigarette. "All right, Quigley," he said in a matter-of-fact tone, "now what is it you want to tell me?"

The abrupt transformation took Quigley completely by surprise. With one deft question, aptly put, Davitt had given Quigley charge of the conversation and made it necessary for him to lead it. He cleared his throat and tossed off his drink, scowling at Davitt as the latter calmly lighted his cigarette.

His eyes narrowed slightly but his gaze became calmly quizzical. "You seem to think I know a whole lot more than I do, Davitt. I guess Lamby has lost some cattle because what would be the sense in him making such a fuss if he didn't have anything to back it up? It's bound to get around that he brought you into this thing, and if he didn't have good reason, he'd only be making a fool out of you, or a fool of himself. I don't think you're dumb enough to let him put anything over on you, and I can't see how it would do him any good."

Davitt was listening intently, and he realized that Quigley was in earnest. "You're not sure he has lost any stock?" he asked.

"Of course I'm not!" Quigley exclaimed. "But I just told you I couldn't see why he should say so unless he has lost some. I've lost some stock, too, but I'm not making any fuss because I think it's strayed. Hull and me are new to the cattle game. Didn't you know that? Hull's always been in sheep. Naturally, Lamby doesn't take to him any too hard. He's always been in cattle. He's hinted that his stock strayed on to our range and got stuck in a gumbo patch and couldn't get out. That's why I'm not sure of anything except that we don't know anything about his cattle."

"You think Lamby's trying to make out that Hull stole some of his cattle because Lamby doesn't like him?" Davitt persisted.

"I'm hinting there might be some feeling because Lamby is a cowman and Hull once was in sheep," replied Quigley steadily. "Naturally I'm sticking up for Hull. But it's possible there might be some rustling going on. I can't take the time right now to find out. From what I've heard, that part of it is going to be up to you.

If I knew anything for sure, I'd be working on the business myself. They say you've had experience in that line and you'll be scouting around in the proper way. I'm not going to put any fool notions into your head, but ..." He ceased talking and stared at his own reflection in the mirror.

"It wouldn't be the first time my head's been full of fool notions," Davitt observed cynically.

Quigley looked at him closely. "Maybe you don't know it all then. Well, they use worms for fishing, and maybe you could use worms as clues. Whether you think that's a joke or not, you won't be liable to forget it, anyway. So long."

Davitt stared for a full minute at the vacant doorway after Quigley had gone out. Then he burst into a loud laugh.

"Barkeep, come here," he invited cheerfully. "We'll take a drink on my hat. I'm hearing through it!"

CHAPTER TWELVE

Buck Granger had hardly gained the sidewalk when he saw the man Davitt had described walking slowly on the side of the street directly across from the hotel. Although he only caught a single flash of the man's eyes, Buck saw with a thrill that there was indeed something peculiar about them. He noted also that the man was short and slight, bowlegged and hunched in appearance. He did not remember having noticed him before.

Buck was careful that the man Davitt had called Screw-eye did not see him looking at him. For that matter, Screw-eye ignored the cowpuncher after that one direct glance. He walked faster than Buck, who strolled down the opposite side of the street, and turned in at the Green Bottle. As he went in the door, pivoting almost on his heel, Buck saw something that he thought had escaped Davitt's notice. When in a hurry, Screw-eye betrayed a slight limp in his left leg. Buck would remember this because the man's left foot would be the one he put first into the stirrup when mounting. Since he was one who had spent most of his life around horses, Buck naturally would remember that Screw-eye would instinctively favor his left leg in taking the saddle. Possibly it would slow the act of mounting.

Recalling what Davitt had told him, Buck felt convinced that the man was spying on them. With the conviction came the desire to act on his own initiative, in his own way. No sooner did he feel this urge than the idea as to how to do so entered his head and invested itself with logical reasoning.

He crossed the street and entered the Green Bottle. With a casual glance about the large room, he sauntered up to the bar and to all appearances found himself accidentally standing next to Screw-eye. The man favored him with a fixed stare that was almost glassy. It gave Buck an uncomfortable sensation and he frowned as he put some silver on the bar and signaled to the man in the white jacket.

"Aren't you the bozo who was standing behind my chair last night when I was trying to make a few dollars with the picture cards?" he asked the man beside him.

"Everybody tries to make a few dollars in a game," was the short reply in a dull voice.

"I never thought of that when I asked you the question," said Buck. "Have a drink as a favor on me so I can ask one from you."

The man nodded to the bartender who put out a bottle and two glasses. "You don't seem to need many favors," he said, indicating Buck's pile of silver.

"Oh, I'm not asking you to trade drinks," explained Buck. "I just want to ask you not to stand behind me when you see me playing again. I'm sort of superstitious that way."

The man flashed him a look in which malevolence lurked. "Your luck wasn't so bad," he rasped. His right hand thumped against the bar with an instinctive motion that was not lost upon Buck.

"You needn't feel riled," Buck said easily. "I've had a run of luck lately and I'm hoping it'll hold out a spell. Next time you feel like looking on, let me know and I'll buy you off." He was watching the man in the mirror behind the bar and was rewarded by seeing the bold-shot eyes flare red for an instant.

"Here's howdy," said the man, tossing off his drink. "You're a cowhand, I take it." His look was like a keen blade.

"Make it top hand and you have it," Buck said soberly.

"You'll make more money on circle than you will gamblin' with cards, or anything else," was the rejoinder, as the man turned away.

Buck put down his glass with a bang. Taking two swift steps, he caught the man by the arm and whirled him about. "That remark will stand explaining," he said curtly. "What was you thinking of, Screw-eye?" He addressed the other by the name Davitt had given him without thinking.

The smaller man's eyes glittered with a fiery green light. "You couldn't buy me off a nothin'!" he snapped savagely. "And don't try to make a show-off by pickin' on me, neither."

As he was about to reply Buck felt a hand on his arm. He looked around and found a tall, rather sleepy-looking man at his side.

"What's the matter, cowboy?" said this individual in a thick voice.

Buck bristled at this interruption. The stranger to all appearances was a cowpuncher who had begun early on a day of celebration. In the interval, Screw-eye had moved aside and returned to lounge against the bar. Buck wondered if the intercession had been intentional.

"You here again?" he said with a lift of his brows. He was trying to place the stranger and the question was a feeler.

"No, I'm here ... yet," stammered the man with a slight cough. "Say, I wanna speak to you a minute. Come into the back room with me and have a beer while we talk medicine?"

"Sure," Buck said instantly, shooting a glance at Screw-eye

who seemed to be negotiating with the bartender. "Can you walk that far?"

"You watch me," said the other in a boastful tone. "They've never put my legs nor my brain to sleep yet. Don't get me wrong, cowboy. There's nothin' the matter with me."

He led Buck to the back room, waving a signal to the bartender on the way. "Sit down," he invited, pointing to a chair at the card table as he dropped into another and sprawled with his left arm on the table. His lids parted wider and his gaze became clearer. "We'll wait till the boy brings in a couple bottles of beer, eh?"

"You don't need much more," frowned Buck. "When's the wedding?"

"Ha!" chuckled the other. "Find the bride! That's good, ain't it? Can't be no weddin' without a bride, eh? Mebbe I'm the missin' bridegroom, eh? Mebbe you are! What's the answer?"

Buck had been racking his brains in an effort to place this stranger, but to no avail. "Do you know me?" he asked suddenly.

"Sure, I know you," was the braying response. "You're Buck Granger, and you're a cowboy … spurs and everything. Am I right?"

There was one window in the room and it was opposite the door. Buck moved his chair around so that he sat where he could see the light from the window full on the man's face. As he did this, he stole a sly glance and saw the other's eyes lighted with interest, the sleepy look gone. It might be that the man was feigning his apparent mild intoxication and if this were true there must be a reason for the ruse.

"Granted you're right," he said cheerfully, "what name are you using now?"

"Trawler," replied the other. "Mebbe you don't know me, eh?"

At this juncture the bartender entered with two bottles of beer and two glasses. As he tipped the caps from the bottles Trawler thrust his right hand into his trousers pocket and drew out a silver dollar that he tossed on the table in payment. In that brief space of time Buck nodded toward Trawler and frowned questioningly at the bartender. He saw the bartender shake his head slightly in the negative, which meant either that he didn't know Trawler or that the man was no good.

Trawler filled his glass a bit unsteadily. "Here's to good grass," he said, blinking at Buck as he gulped the beverage.

"What you got to tell me that's worth listening to?" Buck asked after they had imbibed.

Trawler stretched his left arm on the table and fingered his glass with his right hand, smacking his lips. "You goin' to work soon?" he asked, squinting at the window where the sun blazed.

"When I'm good and ready, which isn't a promise," Buck answered.

"This is important," said Trawler, straightening in his chair with an effort. "You goin' back to work on Payne's ranch?"

"I thought you said you wanted to speak to me." Buck's tone was sharp and cold. "What do you want ... a line of information?"

"Mebbe. Who knows? I've always asked for what I want, and I've usually got it. I've got to ask you a question or two in order to tell you something you might want to hear." Trawler winked sleepily.

"Ask me a hard one and maybe I'll answer it," Buck suggested.

"Heh! Fair enough." Trawler leaned over the table. "Are you figurin' on trailin' with this man hunter that's drifted in here?"

Buck tensed but managed to smile. "Suppose I am?" he parried.

"Bad business!" Trawler exclaimed. "The boys wouldn't like it."

"No?" Buck was keenly interested. "What boys do you mean?"

"Oh ... the boys." Trawler waved his right hand aimlessly. "I'm with Roy Lamby's outfit. Now you see?"

Buck had pricked his ears instantly. If the speaker really was intoxicated he might be telling something not intended for Buck's ears. Otherwise, he might be conveying a subtle warning. There was another point to be considered, but Buck didn't think of it at the time.

"Suppose you come right out and speak what's on your mind, Trawler," said Buck in a louder voice.

Trawler's eyes widened with a look of warning and he wiggled a finger on his puffy lips. "Not so much heat," he cautioned. "I'm talkin' to you and not to the whole town. If you're figgerin' on goin' in with that fellow I mentioned, it wouldn't look good, that's all. Lamby thinks he's losin' cattle, and mebbe he's got an idea where he's losin' 'em, that's all. Let this fellow find out. It ain't no hole where a cowpuncher like yourself would fit in, see?"

It occurred to Buck that the changes in inflection in Trawler's voice as the thickness of his speech gave way occasionally to crisp clarity, and the recurring brilliant flashes in his eyes belied the man's apparent alcoholic condition. He managed to watch Trawler closely without rousing the latter's suspicions. Yet he was unable to determine to his complete satisfaction whether or not the man was shamming.

"Seems to me," drawled Buck, "if it's just a common case of rustling, a cowpuncher would be just as good on the job as anybody else." So Trawler knew that Lamby had hired Davitt. It didn't look as if Lamby could be trying to keep the matter much of a secret.

"Maybe it ain't just common rustlin'," Trawler said with a wink. "If it was, wouldn't Roy send the boys out to clean up the rustlers?"

"How many you got in the outfit?" asked Buck quickly.

Trawler waved his hand again. "Enough," he said with a scowl. "The boys don't like it and mebbe it'll upset the range. It ain't no place for a puncher to be takin' a holiday."

"Did you come in with Lamby?" Buck queried casually.

"No, I'm celebratin' a little on my own hook," growled Trawler, pouring the rest of the beer from his bottle into his glass and tossing it off. "What Lamby does ..." He sputtered and wiped his lips with the back of his hand.

"Just who're you talking for besides yourself, if anyone?"

"For your own good," Trawler blurted. "I don't want to see no cowhand roped into a deal he don't know nothing about, and where he ain't wanted. I'm doin' you a favor by tippin' you off."

"You mean you're trying to scare me off," said Buck sharply. "You're shooting off your mouth about something you don't know anything about, or something that isn't any of your business. Seems funny to me that they can let a man off to go on a bust at a busy time like this." He was looking straight into Trawler's wavering eyes.

"That's another thing that ain't any of your business," sneered Trawler. "You gotta put your nose in, eh? All right, go to it."

He kicked his chair back, but rose unsteadily, his eyes on Buck the while. He stood leaning on his left hand on the table, leering.

Buck was on his feet in an instant. He stepped around and confronted Trawler as the man straightened.

"Something tells me you're not as drunk as you're trying to make me believe," Buck said crisply. "Since you started this, I aim to find out."

His right fist struck with the last word. The blow caught Trawler flush on the chin and sent him back against the table, which tipped, and the man sprawled on a chair, his eyes darting fire.

Buck stepped back, expecting a rush. Even if the man were drunk, the blow had not been hard enough to sober him. Regardless of where Trawler had obtained his information, Buck was convinced now that the man was not connected with Lamby's outfit, for he had evaded direct questions which no cowhand would have hesitated answering. His advice had merely been a threat.

But Trawler didn't rush. He was on his feet with amazing speed, sending the chair spinning out of the way. Buck tensed to leap in for a second blow as Trawler's right hand moved like light and his gun roared and shook the little room. Buck thought the hot breath of the bullet fanned his cheek as he drove a left that glanced off Trawler's head. The gun spoke twice again, and Buck flung himself to one side, his own hand flashing down to his weapon.

Then Buck stood dumbfounded. It seemed to him that Trawler had turned a back-somersault through the open window. The room was empty, save for himself. Trawler was gone. There was the square of sunlight that had swallowed Trawler as if by magic. Buck leaped to the window and looked out. Trawler was not in sight. There were numerous openings in the narrow alley and he could have disappeared into any of these.

Buck hurried out of the room and met the bartender who had come immediately upon hearing the shots.

"Do you know that fellow who called himself Trawler?" Buck demanded.

"No," replied the bartender. "What was the shooting about?"

"He did it," Buck snapped. "Did you ever see him before? How long has he been drinking? Hurry up and tell me, and then keep still to the crowd."

"Never saw him before last night," was the quick answer. "He's been hittin' it up all night and this morning. Nobody hurt?"

"Just my feelings," Buck said, and scowled. "He picked a fight and went out through the window. Tell this mob to forget it."

He pushed his way through the throng that was gathering, his glances searching the place for Screw-eye. But Screw-eye wasn't in the place. With this knowledge, the thought flashed through Buck's mind that Trawler might have drawn him away from Screw-eye to give the latter a chance to get away.

He hurried out of the place and turned instinctively toward the livery on the run. He reached the barn just in time to see a figure swing into the saddle on a horse at the rear. It was a clumsy mount and the rider was of slight build. Buck placed him instantly. It was Screw-eye! Next moment there was a clatter of hoofs and horse and rider were gone.

As Buck turned toward the livery office to ask a question he had a disconcerted feeling of frustration. In all probability, Trawler, too, was gone.

CHAPTER THIRTEEN

It was nearly an hour before Buck turned his steps back toward the hotel where he had left Davitt. He had learned nothing. The day man at the livery had no information to give him and Buck naturally had to exercise great caution in making inquiries. He felt satisfied, however, that there had been a connection between Screw-eye and Trawler, and he was equally certain that the pair had left town.

He looked at the matter coolly, considering the fact that he had been shot at three times by Trawler. If it was true that the man had been indulging all night and morning, this would seem reasonable enough excuse for his faulty work with his pistol. On the other hand, Buck could not bring himself to believe that Trawler had been drunk, and he was not satisfied that he had pursued the proper course in accosting Screw-eye. But the fact that Trawler knew of Davitt's interest in Lamby's trouble was valuable news. So Buck thought, but he was nettled and dissatisfied with his morning's work and had a suspicion that Davitt would not approve of it, which did not serve to soothe his feelings.

To his surprise he found Davitt and Lamby in the lobby of the hotel standing near the door. Lamby smiled at him faintly while Davitt gave him a cold look. Buck's spirits flared in resentment.

"Just a minute, Buck," Davitt said as the cowpuncher was about to pass them. "Lamby and I have been talking and it may be that … I may have to …" He paused with a frown as if groping for words.

"Give up the business or go it alone, I suppose," Buck supplied, looking straight at Lamby who returned his gaze mildly.

"I didn't say that exactly," said Davitt curtly.

"But that's what you meant," Buck retorted hotly. "It's all right with me. I've got a question to ask Lamby, here, just the same."

He turned to the stockman. "Have you got a man working for you by the name of Trawler?" he demanded. "Tall, sandy-looking hand with a mean eye and a quick gun paw?"

"Not that I know of," drawled Lamby. "I'd be more apt to know him by a nickname. But I haven't got any sandys working for me."

"Well, then, did you bring anybody from your outfit in with you?" Buck asked with a glare.

"No," replied Lamby with a puzzled frown. "Would it make very much difference if I had?"

"It might make a lot of difference," Buck snapped out. "Looks to me … but never mind. I know one thing, though … if I had a stock ranch and something was wrong, I'd have to have a mighty good reason before I called in outside help to settle the trouble. Payne wouldn't do it." With this shot Buck walked to the stairs.

"Once a puncher, always a puncher, I reckon," Lamby said in a plaintive voice.

"Yes, I know," said Davitt. "I was one myself once. I'll see what can be done, Mister Lamby. So long."

Lamby went out with a frown on his face. In so many words he had been dismissed. He wasn't used to it, and he didn't like it.

When Davitt entered their room a few minutes later he found

Buck arranging his slicker pack. The cowpuncher threw him an angry glance. Davitt disregarded it, put his hat on the bureau, and flung himself on the bed where the book he had been reading that morning still lay, face down, its pages pressed against the blanket.

Buck was making up his pack on the table and as he saw Davitt pick up the book and settle his head against the propped-up pillows he could stand it no longer.

"So you think I'm excess baggage, do you?" he exploded.

"I was pleased with the way you took the hint," Davitt replied calmly, looking at him in approval. "Your talk impressed Lamby."

"I see, I see," sputtered Buck. "Made your grandstand play good, I reckon. I'm likely to impress Lamby some more before I get through." He turned to the work at hand.

"I said something about temper being dangerous this morning but that didn't seem to impress you, Buck," Davitt said coolly. "What were you shooting those questions at Lamby for, and why was that gent down in the Green Bottle shooting at you?"

Buck's resentment and anger suddenly subsided. "I sort of walked into Screw-eye, and the gent you mention walked into me," he said, taking out his tobacco and papers. "I asked Lamby if he had a man named Trawler working for him because that was the name the shooting gent gave me and his address. I reckon I found out something, at that."

Davitt put down his book as Buck lighted his smoke. "Don't stop your packing," he advised. "It'll look better for you to ride out of town ahead of me. Go ahead and tell me what happened."

Buck took a few thoughtful puffs, staring at Davitt curiously. Then he shrugged his shoulders and went smoothly about his packing, describing the conversations and what had taken place that morning after he had left the hotel.

"If you want to ask me," he concluded," this is a flat cold deck and Mister Roy Lamby is holding the same."

"I'm not so sure." Davitt frowned. "I've seen another party besides Lamby since you've been gone. He was Quigley, who is Matt Hull's foreman. He's another that knew we were going to get tangled up in this thing. If I didn't feel sure that Sylvester Graham egged Lamby into calling us in, and let Hull in the deal, too, so we would be the goats if there were going to be any goats, I wouldn't touch it. Do you know Quigley?"

"No," Buck answered shortly. "The Hull outfit never has mixed in town. He's got all northern hands ... a lot of 'em are Canadians and some are from the eastern part of the state. They've kept to themselves."

"He might feel he wanted a new crew, starting in the cattle game after being in sheep so long," observed Davitt. "Quigley as much as confessed he wasn't an old cowhand. Said Lamby would try to blame Hull because Hull had been a sheep man. Stalled me along trying to get information out of me, and then gave himself away by telling me people used worms for fishing so why shouldn't I use worms as clues." Davitt laughed outright.

"That doesn't sound funny to me," Buck said, wrinkling his eyes. "Sounds as if he was sneering at us ... at you, anyway."

"And that's right where I figured he gave himself away," said Davitt, sobering. "Don't you see, Buck, that there's more to this than just some cattle missing, although the cattle furnish reason enough?"

Buck finished tying his pack. "It looks like an open and shut case to me," growled Buck. "If this Quigley knew Lamby was going to call you in, then he must have got his information from Hull. Where did Hull learn about it? From Old Sylvester, of course. Didn't the mortgage king have the two of 'em handy this morning? He's interested in both parties because they both owe the bank money. He doesn't want 'em fighting between themselves. If my gent, Trawler, didn't get his information from Lamby, then he got it from Quigley. If old Screw-eye is in on it, too, why, the same goes for him. I wouldn't be surprised if Quigley was trying to give you a bum steer in his awkward way."

"I thought of that, too," Davitt said in a serious tone, "but this business is hot. Lamby has lost three hundred head, maybe more. They disappeared from three different herds and all were grazing on the Hull Ranch side. That's the east side of Lamby's Triangle range. Three hundred head of prime stock makes it real rustling."

Buck whistled softly. "Maybe Trawler *did* want to plug me for keeps, after all," he said slowly.

"I wouldn't wonder," Davitt said, nodding. "Lamby heard about the shooting down below just before he came up here. I guess he thought you were in a common jam. I let on I was going to split with you. I have a hunch that five hundred head would be closer to the Triangle's actual losses, for you can bet that Graham wouldn't have called on me unless he knew it was serious."

Buck dropped into a chair with a faint smile. "It takes team-work somewhere for that many cows or steers to be blotted out. Whoever is behind this isn't afraid of powder smoke, that's a cinch."

"I wouldn't be surprised if we smelled some before we're through," said Davitt earnestly. "You know, Buck, I've been think-ing. You're a good fellow, you're solid down at the Payne Ranch, you've got a decent stake in the bank. This looks like straight range work. You don't have to go in on this. I ... well, I don't know just how to put in so many words what I've got in my mind."

"No?" Buck raised his brows. "I thought you learned how to talk by reading books. Here, you've got something to say, and you're stuck. I don't aim to embroider my words any, but I'm usually able to think up some that mean what I think and string 'em out." He nodded airily.

Davitt smiled wryly. "There's three trails to Triangle, Lamby told me," he said, looking straight ahead over the foot of the bed at the wall. "One trail starts at the upper end of the main street and is a road that leads straight to the Lamby Ranch. The other starts at the end of the cross street, north of the bank. That's a fair road, too, and goes along the boundary between the Triangle and the Hull Ranch. The other trail heads off northwest by way of Horseshoe Butte, and cuts into the rough country up there into a corner of Hull's range where it first touches the Triangle." He paused and glanced at the cowpuncher, who was listening with the patient air of a man who is hearing something he already knew.

"After sundown," Davitt continued, "I'm going to ride out on one of those trails. Suppose you think this matter over carefully, Buck, and then, if you decide you want to, meet me after dark. It'll be up to you to guess which trail I'm going to take. If there should be anybody watching, I'd like to have 'em see you ride out for the south while it's still broad day."

Buck looked at him squarely. "You're giving me a chance to back out in a nice, respectable, easy way," he drawled. "It's sort of white of you, Mel, at that. You think this business is going to be red-hot. Why should I risk my hide? I'd quit this minute if I thought you'd say you would rather work by yourself. No? I thought so. Sure you don't feel sore about my party this morning?"

"I told you to use your own judgment as to rules when it was necessary," frowned Davitt. "You stumbled into two outsiders in this mess."

Buck grinned. "Maybe they're both on the inside," he said, hefting his pack. "I'll ride along and see if I can figure out the trail you'll take. Don't forget it's hard riding round by Horseshoe Butte."

There was just a flicker of Mel Davitt's lids. Then he swung out of the bed and took Buck's hand.

"If I never see you again, it'll be soon enough!" he cried in a voice that anyone near might hear.

CHAPTER FOURTEEN

It was later afternoon when Mel Davitt appeared on the street, neatly dressed in a double-breasted blue suit, his youthful and cheerful appearance at total variance with his reputation for being cool, calculating, and dangerous. His eyes sparkled as he nodded amicably to those who spoke to him whether they knew him or not. He was aware that Buck had eaten his dinner hurriedly and had left town immediately. Through the good offices of the hotel clerk and the liveryman he had ascertained that Lamby, Hull, and Quigley had also departed. He thus had the present field to himself.

He sauntered down the street and half an hour before its closing time he stepped into the State Bank of Milton. He walked briskly back to the door of Sylvester Graham's private office, rapped smartly, and entered upon the banker's curt invitation.

Graham showed surprise and glanced at his visitor's attire with apparent disapproval. Davitt sat in a chair across the desk from Graham and put his hat on his knee. His smile was confident.

"What's the matter? Aren't you going to look into the Lamby trouble?" asked the banker with a frown.

"I promised Lamby I would and I believe I told you so," Davitt said easily. "First of all, I believe the sheriff and the Cattlemen's Association should be notified that I'm working on the case so there can be no interference."

"I'll look after that," Graham said crisply. "I explained this morning that you needn't have any misgivings on that score."

"But you didn't tell me how many cattle were missing."

"Didn't Lamby tell you?" flared the banker.

"He told me a hundred here in your office, but then later I learned from him that it probably was a lot more."

Graham's eyes popped. "Did Lamby tell you that?" he demanded.

"Lamby said the amount was more like three hundred. So when he jumps his original figure to three times as much, I feel that even the new figure is probably too low. This isn't any petty little spite rustling deal, Mister Graham, and you knew that in the first place. Otherwise, why should you make sure I was asked to take a hand? You know I don't bother with small stuff."

"I recommended you because I didn't want any hullabaloo on the range," Graham snapped at him. "That's why I don't want the sheriff's office, or the association outfit mixed up in it. I really didn't know it was quite so ... ah ... big." A single gleam of worry showed in his eyes.

"Well, you know now. The name of Lamby's ranch fits this problem exactly. It's a triangle with the usual three angles. One angle is the Lamby Ranch, another is the Hull Ranch, and the third is this office. Lamby has money borrowed on the missing stock, hasn't he?"

"That's between Lamby and the bank," Graham replied shortly.

"And between the bank and me," Davitt said with a sharp edge to his words. "You want this stock recovered, do you not? Every head of stock that's lost puts that much more money loaned on his other cattle, doesn't it? You don't want any more stolen, do you?"

"Lamby has ample security for any loans he has outstanding."

"Sure. But how about Hull? If he found he had a few hundred head more than he thought he had, he wouldn't kick, would he? He does business with you, does he not?"

"Great Scott! You don't suspect Hull, do you?" Graham asked, startled.

"Why not?" demanded Davitt. "He's a sheep man at heart, isn't he? There isn't any love lost between him and Lamby, is there? It isn't too much to think he might grab some of Lamby's stock if he had it in for him, is it?"

"I don't believe it," Graham said with a formidable frown. "Now I'll tell you something. Lamby wanted your services to avoid any trouble with Hull. There's been some feeling, I'll admit, but I know Hull wouldn't think of stealing any of Lamby's stock. He couldn't get away with any cattle because this bank will have a representative at his roundup."

"Ah. So he is into the bank pretty deep. You didn't tell me as much, but I'll consider it a confidence. It doesn't look to me as though he could afford to steal stock and get rid of it on the sly. On the other hand, wouldn't it be possible for Lamby to shove some cows on Hull's range and claim they had been stolen?"

"He couldn't get away with it," snorted Graham. "And besides, he's a cattleman and always has been one. A real cattleman doesn't do such tricks."

"No? Well, you'd sure be surprised at some of the tricks I've known 'em to pull, and I've never seen one yet that would reason when it came to sheep or in dealing with anybody mixed up with sheep. I think Lamby lied about the number of cattle he's lost, and if he'll lie about that, he'll lie about other things. One point I'm sure of … if it was just a case of outside rustling, the range would rise up and drive the outlaws out. It can be done."

Having delivered himself of this speech, Davitt rose as if to go.

"Sit down a minute," Graham said earnestly. "I may as well tell you that the bank is interested in this. Every stockman has to borrow money and we're here to lend it. Naturally we expect to get it back with interest. If there was a big rustling scare right now it would attract rustlers clear from the border. Now you know another reason why I want to go at this business quietly. I really don't know what inside conditions are. That's why I recommended you."

The banker tapped his desk with his fingers and looked Davitt squarely in the eyes as he finished.

"That's saying a straight mouthful," said Davitt. "Is there anything else you can tell me that'll help me to figure this thing out? I haven't got much to work on, you know."

"Not a thing," Graham replied soberly.

"You don't believe Hull knows anything about the rustling?"

"I don't believe he knows a thing about it. I have a way to make him tell if he knows anything. Between you and me, he has everything to lose and nothing to gain by making trouble on this range."

Davitt rose again from his chair. "All right," he said crisply, his eyes narrowing, "now I'll tell you something. It isn't any baby outfit of amateurs that's stealing these cattle. They mean business. There's going to be shooting of the worst kind before this is over. If anybody concerned is holding anything back from me, or tries to put anything over on me, he'll find himself on the wrong end, that's all."

"I hear there's been shooting already," Graham said with a frown.

"A barroom misunderstanding," scoffed Davitt.

"I hear, too, that you've split with that upstart puncher, Granger," said Graham, giving Davitt a keen look. "He could make a mess of things easy enough."

"Things will make a mess of themselves without any help," Davitt said mysteriously. "Did Hull tell his foreman, Quigley, about my being asked to take a hand?"

"He probably did. Quigley's been with him a long time."

"Well, it's a nice day," Davitt said, as he left the office.

He went out of the bank with a grim smile playing on his lips. From the banker he had learned the sum total of nothing, in so far as a hint indicating who might be stealing the cattle was concerned. He had merely verified his suspicions that both Lamby and Hull were into the bank for heavy loans, and that it was Graham who had suggested that he be called in in the first place because the banker wished to protect his collateral and do so without disturbing the range in general. This could hardly be called selfish on Graham's part. It was good business at the expense of the stockmen. Yet something in Lamby's manner had convinced Davitt that he had acceded to Graham's demands unwillingly. Davitt was annoyed because he could not put his finger definitely on a clue. Everything was under cover, unless Buck had stumbled into something that morning. But Davitt was of determined caliber.

He returned to the room in the hotel. He could not shake off the feeling that invisible eyes had noted his movements. But as he was a stranger in the town he could not distinguish other strangers from habitants or regular frequenters of the place. Although he had kept his eyes alert, he had seen nothing of Screw-eye, nor anyone answering the description Buck had given him of Trawler. He stood still in the center of the room struck by the realization that he actually missed Buck Granger. For several years Davitt had been a lone rider. He had welcomed the companionship of the jovial, happy cowpuncher. He was conscious of an inward glow of supreme satisfaction that his first estimate of Buck had been correct. For Buck was honest and frank, fearless and capable, with many of Davitt's own devil-may-care characteristics, and—most important of all—Buck possessed a delicious sense of humor.

Davitt had not felt altogether comfortable about drawing Buck into an adventure which might prove exceedingly dangerous. He had opened the way for the cowpuncher to decide that a good stake in the bank, and a steady place, with an excellent chance for promotion, was better than being with him in a dangerous undertaking, the outcome of which was far from certain. He half hoped that Buck would give up thought of participation in the enterprise. But there was a wistful look in Davitt's eyes as he considered this.

"He knows, doggone him, that I'm going to take the Horseshoe trail," Davitt muttered, looking about vacantly. "It's the worst of the three ways to the Triangle range, and the badlands are a natural hideout. He knew I was testing him with the we're-quits bluff. I wonder if I'll meet him."

His eyes flashed clear and a stern look came to his face. A different Davitt than had sauntered down to the bank a short time before. He turned to his open pack, spread out on the floor. From it he took his cartridge belt and gun and cleaning kit and put them on the table. Then he changed his clothes.

The neat blue suit was switched for a black sateen shirt, dark trousers, heavier socks. The polished riding boots were put aside for a worn pair, pulled on over his pants bottoms. Spurs now jingled when he stepped about. A blue silk scarf was substituted for the cravat he had worn. A Stetson that had seen hard service replaced the elegant beaver-plush headpiece that had won such admiration.

Davitt sat down by the table and carefully cleaned and oiled his gun. He spun the cylinder until it seemed on ball bearings. He fanned the hammer until it almost appeared as a shadow. And finally, he fondled it, slid it back and forth in the palm of his hand, admiring its balance, and slipped it into its holster.

He put his yellow slicker aside and wrapped his clothes carefully in a piece of thin canvas, carried for the purpose. This he would leave for safekeeping in the hotel. Done up in his slicker would be only some sandwiches and other emergency food and some coffee and sugar, and extra cartridges and his cleaning kit. He would travel light.

And all this time, while he went about his preparations with methodical thoroughness, his brain was busy. There was no place in his thoughts for anything of a trivial nature. Worms as clues, indeed. Davitt's lips tightened firmly.

At six o'clock he went down to supper. After the meal he went to the livery and made sure of the directions to Lamby's ranch house. The road swung north at the west end of the main street, as he already knew. He made inquiries in the event that word of his going, and his direction, would be given out.

The twilight was blending into night when he rode out of town at a canter. He turned up trail number one and put his mount to a swinging lope. He kept close watch over his shoulder but glimpsed no pursuing shadow. Five miles out on the north road he swung east across the open plain in a spurt. He crossed trail number two, the dim road which led to the boundary between the Triangle and the Hull range. Then he swerved a bit south and in another half hour picked up the trail that wound up the snaky course of the stream and then veered northeast toward the shadow of Horseshoe Butte, which loomed dimly against the low-hanging stars.

He got off his horse presently and examined the trail, even feeling of it with his open hand. It would not be good policy to light a match to look more closely. But he was certain the fresh tracks left by a horse were there. He mounted swiftly and sped at a fast pace.

The level prairie became disturbed and rolled with occasional dips into shallow washes and coulees which the trail skirted. Ridges appeared. Horseshoe frowned closer. The sky was studded with stars but there was no moon. The shadows danced, gathered, and broke apart as he surmounted the rises, formed blots in the washes, black streaks in the narrow deep ravines. Clumps of trees and willows appeared in the occasional wet places. The going became rough.

Then, far ahead, two pinpoint flashes of red winked.

Davitt leaned forward and shook out his reins. His horse broke into a gallop.

CHAPTER FIFTEEN

Buck Granger trotted out of town on the south road shortly after high noon. He wore his hat at a saucy angle over his right eye, whistled merrily, and to all appearances was headed for his home ranch after an enjoyable and profitable holiday. In truth Buck was in excellent humor. He had surmised almost from the moment when Davitt had first addressed him in the lobby before Lamby that Davitt was simulating displeasure for effect. Davitt didn't want the town at large to know that Buck was associated with him in the new job. It was just as well, Buck decided, to keep the public in the dark as to their movements. He had sufficient faith in Davitt to respect the latter's notions. He grinned when he thought of the clumsy way in which Davitt had given him an opportunity to back out. He sensed that Davitt didn't want him to do any such thing, and it went without saying that he had no such intentions. The very fact that Davitt might possibly be worried about the outcome of the rustling investigation convinced Buck that Davitt expected fast and dangerous work. The reckless light of wild adventure sparkled in Buck's eyes. He even whistled cheerfully, and his horse caught this spirit of wild abandon, pricked up its ears, and pranced like a thoroughbred.

Buck laughed with sheer delight. "Horse, you won't feel like dancing before this trick is over, or the buckaroo who's forking you will miss his guess," he sang.

The horse single-footed prettily down the dusty road. Buck looked back through the golden, spinning dust spirals to where the green setting of the town was shading to a drab gray in the brilliant sunshine as the distance lengthened. He was looking for a telltale dust cloud that might indicate that he was being followed. But the town's shadow was blotted out and faded from view, with no such signal appearing.

With no one in sight, Buck increased his pace and galloped along the verdant banks of the stream. He stopped whistling and smiling, and the alert light in his eyes changed to a look of eagerness. Buck was familiar with almost every square mile of the north range and he thought with no small measure of satisfaction that Davitt, who was a stranger in the district, needed his services as guide. Presently he came to stony ground where the shod hoofs of his horse struck fire from small rocks and raised no dust. His gaze now was fixed on the trees that lined the banks of the stream. He grunted with satisfaction when he saw a rift of horizon blue through the leafy branches. He turned abruptly off the road and soon was in a gravel-floored gully riding down, hugging his horse's neck, with the branches arching over him. Soon he splashed through the shallow waters of a ford in the stream with hard footing underneath.

As he rode up the steep sandy bank on the opposite side he came into a clear, grassy space among some twisted thorn-apple trees. Here he drew rein, dismounted, and tossed the loose reins over his horse's head to dangle while the animal grazed. With the natural respect of a top hand for his favorite mount's well-being and comfort, he loosened the single cinch of his stock saddle. Then Buck proceeded to lighten his slicker pack by doing his town clothes up in a neat bundle, using some newspapers for a wrapper, and tying the pack with a rawhide thong. He secreted the pack in a miniature rock cave in the bank of the stream.

"And if a chipmunk gives 'em to a muskrat, I won't be losing much," he said aloud gaily.

Next, he folded some food rations he had brought along into his slicker and tied it to the rear of his saddle. His trail preparations completed, he sat down on a tuft of bunch grass and leaned comfortably against the trunk of a cottonwood. From this position he could see through the rift in the line of trees and glimpse any rider who might come along the road from any direction.

A man bred and raised in primitive open country possesses the soothing faculty of communing with nature and his own soul without wearisome brain effort or conscious perception of the passage of time. As proof of this an Indian never had need of a sedative. Instead of worrying his mind with conjectures and deductions having to do with the work at hand, Buck lapsed into a reverie, rolling and puffing and relighting brown-paper cigarettes while the sun slipped down the serrated peaks of the western mountains. During those hours the only activity he saw on the road was a passing buckboard bearing some rancher homeward. At sunset he ate two sandwiches of cold beef between thick slices of bread and refreshed himself at a spring that trickled into the stream. Then he watered his horse, tightened his saddle cinch, and struck out of the trees across the undulating reaches of prairie to the Horseshoe Butte trail.

When the twilight lost its seductive purple and deepened into night with the first stars scattered like glowing lanterns in the sky, Buck found himself some miles northwest of the point where the east road led out of town. He had seen no one. He had not expected to meet Davitt this early, yet he had seen what he assumed were fresh tracks in the trail he was following. Either Davitt had passed that way ahead of him, which he doubted, or another rider was making for the Horseshoe country. This last possibility aroused Buck's natural instinct for caution.

In traversing the washes, where his horse's hoofs echoed dully on the hard gumbo, and in skirting the shadowy depths of ravines and coulees, he drew his gun and held it close to him between the pommel of his saddle and his waist, where it could not easily be seen but would be ready for instant action. He rode slowly now, walking his horse. This was to give Davitt quick opportunity of overtaking him.

Although he had left the stream, he was really cutting across an area of broken prairie lying in a great bend of the same stream that curved around to the east toward the opening in Horseshoe Butte. He could see the dark band of shadow made by the trees along the banks of the river directly ahead, with the black bulk of the butte looming behind it. The point where the stream swung in below the butte marked the beginning of a rugged, tumbled district known as the badlands. Here the river flowed down from due north, passing a mile west of the butte near the southwestern corner of Hull's range.

As Buck approached the river slowly he came to a long, gradual ascent where the prairie climbed up to the line of trees. He could barely make out the thin ribbon of trail, but the footing was sound on the path worn through the grass. He had climbed halfway, when, after a searching glance at the shadowy waste behind, he urged his horse on up the ascent at a fast pace.

He could feel the muscles and strong body of his gallant mount bunch and heave under him as the horse lunged forward and literally cleared the remaining distance in a series of mighty bounds. As he reached the top of the rise, Buck's gun was out and held close on his left side under his left arm.

He had scarcely reached the level when he brought his horse

to a quick stop and gave vent to a smothered exclamation. On the left the line of trees was broken, the bank of the stream was clear and fell away in a sheer drop of ten feet or more to a wide pool. Above the pool the water seemed barely moving and alive with silver spangles that reflected the light of the stars. On the edge of the steep bank an object which Buck had thought to be a stump, or a rock of fantastic contour proved to be the silhouette of a man. He was sitting with his legs dangling over the edge of the cliff, a slender rod in his hands, and as Buck caught the flash of the nickel reel he realized the man was fishing.

Buck stared with open-mouthed wonder. Such fishing as he himself had done had been of an early morning or evening and he had invariably used artificial flies. But he had heard of large trout being caught at night, particularly on starlit nights, with a baited hook.

The profile of the fisherman disappeared as the man turned to look at him, and Buck noted he was short, slender, and slightly hunched. Buck walked his horse forward a few paces and slipped from the saddle, still keeping his gun concealed.

He walked close to the fisherman and broke into a short laugh.

"Catching anything, Screw-eye?" he asked in a tone of deliberate derision. He noted that from his position the man had a view of the slope that led up to the high bank of the river. Thus, while Screw-eye, for it was indeed the spy Davitt had suspected, could see the approach of a rider, he could not make his escape readily without showing himself in the act.

"My luck ain't as good as yours," was the sneering answer.

Buck had already decided that the man's presence was not a mere coincidence. Now he decided to take a chance on Screw-eye being identified in some way with the rustling operations. To his way of thinking, any unusual happening might furnish the source for a clue. Since Screw-eye was there, it was not unreasonable, so he figured, to assume that Trawler also was in the vicinity.

"You fishing for something to eat or just for pastime?" he asked.

"G'wan chase your cows," said the man in a vicious voice. "What you sneaking around in the night for, eh?"

For answer Buck stooped quickly and jerked the rod from the man's grasp, using his left hand and glancing quickly about the open space. He pulled the line out of the water and a baited hook dangled in the cold light of the stars.

"You're not faking, at that," Buck growled, throwing down the rod. "How come everywhere I go I find you squatting around?"

The man leaned back on his hands, his eyes glowing green and then sparking red as he looked up at Buck.

"You clumsy fool!" he got out, with an added curse.

In a flash Buck picked up the rod, broke it across his knee, and threw it over the cliff, the reel flying through the air with the line singing shrilly as it spun.

"I guess you were faking, at that," he said sternly. "Where's your camp? Show it to me or I'll drag you around by the collar till I find it."

The man bunched and literally flung himself into the air, his gun glinting in the starlight. But Buck had closed in on him in a twinkling and now his own weapon blazed almost in Screw-eye's face. The man dropped his six-shooter as he felt the hot breath of pistol flame, and Buck's gun blazed again.

Screw-eye staggered back, his features ghastly in the weird light that shone from the illuminated heavens. His hand went quickly over his thin face and he looked at it. When he saw no blood, he rubbed his face again and stared at his hand with his jaw sagging. Then his eyes went red as he gave Buck a look in which baffled rage and intense hatred struggled for mastery.

Buck was laughing coldly, his glances darting about the open space and back to the slope. He had fired for three reasons: to startle Screw-eye into dropping his gun; to bring anyone out who might be with the man; and to attract the attention of Davitt, who, he had reason to believe, was not far behind him on the trail since he had ridden slowly on purpose.

"Back into the trees!" Buck commanded. "Hop along, or the next time I won't fire to scare you. You're not hurt. Get a move on!"

He grasped Screw-eye with his left hand and hurled him into the shadows, bounding after him just as the man whistled so sharply that the shrill signal cut the still air with the reverberating violence of an unexpected thunderclap.

Next instant the man's left hand had gripped Buck's gun wrist like a band of steel and his other hand found the cowpuncher's throat, the fingers shutting off his wind with the painful, merciless, viselike clutch of mighty talons.

The unexpected nature of the ferocious attack, the sudden twist of his wrist, caused Buck to release his hold of the gun. He tore at the fingers in his throat with his left hand, drove his right knee into his adversary's stomach, and literally boosted the man up and over his shoulder.

But his antagonist kept his hold!

Both went to the ground on their backs with Buck partly on top of his attacker, his neck twisted under his own left arm. His head seemed swelling, roaring. The stars over them began to bunch into great fiery balls, swimming in all the colors of the rainbow. His strength was ebbing, and it drove him into a frenzy. Not for one fleeting instant would he have suspected that the man who had him in his power possessed such strength. The sweat stood out on him as he realized it was the strength of a madman he was battling.

Buck rolled over, putting his weight on his attacker's right arm. His left hand found one of the other's ears and he twisted it with all the strength left in him. A hoarse cry came from Screw-eye's throat and his hands went limp. Buck broke away, lights dancing before his eyes. He stood unsteadily looking down at the figure on the ground.

Screw-eye lay motionless. His eyes were open, but his face was the ghostly hue of chalk. His breath came in gulps. Then he began to twitch—first his lips and eyelids, then his hands and arms and legs. Finally his whole body shook as if he were afflicted with a fit of ague.

Buck was unable to take his eyes from this queer sight as his head cleared and the strength surged back into his muscles. In time Screw-eye stopped twitching and shaking and closed his eyes only to open them suddenly and sit bolt upright.

"What happened?" he gasped out, wiping his lips with a hand.

Buck swore softly, uncertainly. Had the man really been temporarily insane or in the throes of a seizure? Was the peculiar light in his eyes indicative of mental instability?

These questions remained unanswered, for Buck suddenly heard a deep, thick voice behind him.

"What's the matter? Did he throw a twister?"

Buck whirled and met the cold, evil-lighted eyes of his assailant of the morning—the man who called himself Trawler.

CHAPTER SIXTEEN

For several moments Buck stood motionless and silent, regarding Trawler with a steady gaze in which there was neither alarm nor surprise. But in that brief space of time Buck thought faster than ever before in his life. Screw-eye and Trawler were undoubtedly companions, and the latter's question tended to show that Screw-eye was subject to fits. Indeed, if the man were mentally unbalanced, it might account for his presence on the bank fishing. But his position had also been an excellent lookout, and Trawler had said he was working for Lamby, a statement which the stockman had failed to confirm. Indeed, if Trawler were working for Lamby, why should he be in this desolate spot off the Triangle range? Buck decided to try the two of them out.

"I reckon he did," he answered. "He made a jump for me when I stopped to talk with him and tried to choke me to death. Friend of yours?"

"Oh, everybody in these parts knows Phelps," said Trawler with a derogatory gesture. "He gets that way from livin' alone. He's a hermit. What you doin' up this way?"

"I'm heading toward the Sweetgrass country, no thanks to

you," replied Buck coldly. "Lucky for me the drinks were behind your aim this morning."

Trawler chuckled. "I was afraid I might have hit you," he said. "I even took a roundabout way home, figurin' I could get over it before I hit the ranch and get the bad news beforehand if there was any. I'm glad to see you're jake. Where's your gun?"

Buck had already glimpsed the reflection of the dull metal of his weapon in the starlight. He walked a few paces and picked the gun up from where it had fallen in the grass. He slipped it into his holster and turned to find Trawler covering him.

Buck never batted an eyelash. He surveyed Trawler coldly. "What's the answer?" he demanded. As he put the question he glanced past Screw-eye, who Trawler had called Phelps, and saw the slope was clear. He knew if Davitt had seen the flashes made by the gun, or had heard the reports, he would be cautious. He had been assured by the look in Davitt's eyes and the flutter of his lids that Davitt had planned to take the Horseshoe trail. The fact that he hadn't said as much in so many words was part of Davitt's clumsy plan to give Buck an opportunity to withdraw from the venture with good excuse if he wished.

"I started to test you out this mornin' to see what you and that four-flusher you were travelin' with were up to," said Trawler in a mean voice. "As a matter of fact, I'm workin' on the Lamby business myself. You busted into me for no reason a-tall except to make me think you was tough. You didn't like the idea of my workin' for Lamby and, for all I know, you knew I was trackin' in this game on my own hook. I'm not lettin' you go till I'm sure of you, that's all, and it won't be healthy for you to kick up any disturbance. You may as well know I didn't intend to shoot you. I pulled that play to throw you off of any play you had in mind. If you hadn't run into Phelps here, I'd have followed you. Now I'm just naturally goin' to hold you tight till I know more about you."

"You can't even talk like you was telling the truth," Buck snorted. "But if I'm wrong, it won't be the first time."

"If you're wrong it may be the last time," Trawler shot back. "Phelps! Get your gun and cover this gent."

Phelps did as he was told, and when he had drawn a steady bead on Buck's heart, Trawler stepped around the puncher and took his gun.

"Funny you'd let me pick it up," Buck said jeeringly.

"I wouldn't bother lookin' for it," said Trawler crossly. "Now just lead your horse along behind Phelps. Go ahead, Phelps … go to the cabin. Step careful, cowboy … if you slip I'm bound to hit you once out of six shots." He laughed as if he considered this a great joke.

But Buck knew he wasn't joking. Moreover, a doubt had assailed the cowpuncher. It might be that Trawler was trailing rustlers. Buck didn't believe the man suspected him as being involved in the cattle thefts, but he might be taking precautions against competition. After all, Lamby hadn't said anyone else was working on the case. Buck was puzzled and mad. And worst of all, he was helpless to do anything about it. He took up his reins and started afoot after Phelps, leading his horse.

The trail led directly through a stand of timber and Buck could see a narrow ribbon of starlit sky that split the deep shadow ahead. As they approached this opening, it widened, as an aisle leading into the nave of a church. Suddenly a huge mass of rock loomed on the right and Phelps turned in close to this rock.

"Push right along behind him," came the order from Trawler.

Buck did so and as they went halfway around the rock they struck into another trail with a sandy bottom where the horses hoofs made no sound. This by-trail led over a ridge, across a gravel-strewn gully, through some scattered firs, and brought up beside a small stream where there was a cabin almost underneath an overhanging bank, or cliff, where the knotted roots of trees showed below the undermined soil like huge ropes. Buck realized that this was a place that would be hard to find, unless one came across the little stream and followed it up.

Phelps was fussing at the door of the cabin. Trawler stood near Buck, who had halted and was holding his horse.

"When he makes a light, go on in," Trawler told him. "I'll look after your horse."

Buck's eyes had accustomed themselves to the dim light and he saw a crude corral under the cutbank where were two horses that most likely belonged to Trawler and Screw-eye, or Phelps, as Buck now knew him.

Phelps made a light and Buck entered the cabin. Phelps stood by the small table on which was the lamp and motioned Buck to the bunk with his gun that he held ready in his right hand.

"Not so fresh now, eh?" Phelps croaked, his bulging eyes snapping.

Buck sat down on the bunk and looked about the small room in amazement, which quickly changed to an expression of disgust. In the corners, under the table, and everywhere on the floor except in front of the small stove and a space between the table and the bunk, was a litter of innumerable objects, including old pack saddles, broken straps, empty bottles, odd bits of leather, gunny sacks, wooden stirrups, discarded clothing, cast-off hats and worn boots, limp tobacco sacks, an overturned pail and a lantern minus its glass chimney, sticks of firewood, yellowed newspapers and magazines, ends and pieces of rope, and a conglomeration of junk that represented the sum total of nothing so far as value or usefulness was concerned.

The cowpuncher looked up from his survey and eyed Phelps with a feeling of repulsion. If the interior of the cabin should be taken as evidence, the man was crazy. Buck surmised that this was what the man Trawler wanted him to believe. Buck noticed two cane fishpoles resting on nails driven in the logs above the window. Phelps, then, was given to fishing on the riverbank after dark. But Buck could not forget that the place where he had found Phelps fishing was a vantage point from which an excellent view of the slope and rugged country below could be obtained. It was not at all unlikely that Phelps had been stationed there as a lookout and Buck had burst in upon him before he could make his escape. Trawler undoubtedly had heard the two shots and had come on the run from the cabin. Had Davitt heard them, too? Buck felt confident that Davitt would find him regardless of the blind entrance to the trail to the cabin. But there lingered the uneasy possibility that Davitt had started later than he had expected, or that some unforeseen contingency had sent him out on one of the other two trails to the Triangle Ranch.

"Build a fire and make some coffee," said Buck suddenly.

Phelps took a step toward the stove and then whirled. The look in his eyes was steel-blue and clear as crystal. "You goin' to give *me* orders?" he shouted wildly.

Buck laughed. "There's nothing the matter with you except you've got ears like a rat," he said with a look of contempt.

"I'd as lief plug you as not!" shrilled Phelps, waving the gun.

"Why don't you?" asked Buck coldly. "Stop juggling that gun."

At this juncture Trawler stepped into the cabin. He frowned at Buck and motioned to Phelps. "Let's have some coffee," he growled.

He pulled a homemade stool up beside the bunk and sat down. "Where's your pal?" he asked, favoring Buck with a searching gaze.

"I dunno," replied Buck, "if it's the one I think you mean."

"He'll be taken care of," Trawler said, his voice full of meaning.

"Sure. Lamby will see to that. He makes his deals in advance."

Trawler's face darkened. "Do you ever stop to think that you maybe don't know as much as you think you do?" he asked. "It was pretty dumb of you to follow us, and it couldn't do you any good. You're not sure this minute what it's all about. You've just stumbled into somethin' and you don't know what it is. You don't even realize that Phelps, here, is dangerous. I heard you baitin' him before I came in." He shot a look at Phelps, who was busying himself at the stove preparing the coffee.

"He took me unawares," Buck said wryly. He looked at Trawler closely. "Am I to understand that I'm a prisoner and being threatened?"

"Not in the strict sense of the word," Trawler returned. "But I'm not goin' to have you chasin' around the country, blunderin' into places where you don't belong and maybe gettin' yourself shot up and me gettin' the blame for it." He scowled darkly, but Buck caught the glimmer of evil cunning in its depths.

"Why not let Phelps take the blame?" he drawled, throwing a dangerous challenge into the man's face.

Trawler swore, and his brutal jaw snapped shut. "By snakes, I'll just leave you with Phelps for safekeepin'," he said.

Buck glanced instinctively toward the figure at the stove and unexpectedly met Phelps' eyes. He shivered involuntarily and turned his gaze away. He experienced a creepy feeling as if he had been momentarily in the spell of a snake. For the first time he was conscious of a definite sensation of misgiving. It struck him like a blow in the face that he could be done away with in this desolate spot and all traces of his disappearance concealed. So Trawler thought he had followed them, and he thought that Davitt had followed him in turn. Since Trawler was wrong, why couldn't he be wrong himself? He shifted on the bunk uneasily.

Phelps gave them each a hot cup of coffee and a cold biscuit. Trawler sipped his coffee and munched the biscuit. Buck followed his example. Phelps was swallowing noisily at the table and Buck knew without looking that the man's eyes were fixed on him. The coffee warmed him, and his confidence gradually returned to a degree. But he didn't like the situation he found himself in even a little bit.

After eating the biscuit and emptying his cup, Trawler got to his feet. He put the cup on the table, wiped his lips with the back of his hand, and pointed to Buck.

"Keep him here till I come back," he said to Phelps.

He slapped the holster on his left with his right hand and stepped to the door. There he peered into the darkness. Buck heard the night wind whistling through rock crevices and swishing with an unnatural sound in the scanty tree growth. Trawler looked at him curiously as if he never expected to see him again and went out.

Buck had made no attempt to hold Trawler since he thought it would be easier to cope with one, even though that one might be crazy, than with two. Now, as he watched Phelps gurgling the dregs of his coffee, his eyes dancing brighter than ever, it struck him that if Trawler intended to keep him a prisoner, alive, it was peculiar that he hadn't bound him hand and foot, so he would be helpless. True, he was unarmed, but he had the use of his hands. Suddenly he started and stared straight at Phelps, the lids narrowed over his eyes. He had been left unbound for a reason. Trawler expected him to try to overpower Phelps and the latter was expected to kill him at the first move.

The cowpuncher's whole body went cold at the thought. Possibly Phelps was deranged. Trawler evidently had some hold over him, for the hermit, so-called, obeyed him meekly enough. Instantly Buck remembered the significant way in which Trawler had slapped his holstered gun. He stared in fascination at Phelps' weapon, which sat on the table close to the man's right hand, its long, cold-blue muzzle pointed in Buck's direction. He might have imagined it, but he thought he saw a gloating, maniacal gleam in the hermit's eyes, which, as Davitt had said, looked like glistening buttons screwed in his head.

At this moment Buck heard a sudden clatter of hoofs on the rocks and the snort of a horse. Trawler was riding away. Buck nearly dropped his cup as a laugh sounded on the wind—short and harsh, and jeering. It might have been the cry of an owl, but Buck smiled grimly. Next there was merely the wind, and the sibilant sucking of Phelps' lips.

Buck gulped the remainder of his coffee. The time to act was before Phelps would reasonably expect it. Where was Trawler going? Buck's place was on the trail where Davitt would pass, the trail that Trawler had probably taken. Buck had an uncanny feeling that he was sitting in the presence of impending death. The youth within him rebelled. He looked at a pile of rags on the floor near the head of the bunk so that Phelps could not see the look in his eyes. As chance would have it, his gaze centered on a thin, iron shaft that stuck out of the nondescript heap—a branding iron.

Buck's mind clicked to a decision.

"How about another cup of coffee?" he said, managing to look up with a grin.

Phelps looked at him coldly, put down his cup, and rested his hand on his gun. "Coffee won't do you any good," he croaked in a horrible voice. "You want something to eat. Dirt's what you want to eat! You want to gnaw roots ... grass roots. Only you're goin' to take what roots you get!" The laugh that rang through the room sent chills up Buck's spine.

Buck nodded toward the stove. "Shall I get it?" he asked.

Phelps did exactly what Buck had expected. He looked at the coffee pot on the stove. In the fraction of a second that the man's gaze was distracted, Buck hurled the cup. It struck Phelps full in the face as Buck leaped for the branding iron. He grasped it, still looking at Phelps, when the latter fired blindly. Buck's body went hurtling across the short intervening space and the twisted brand end of the iron came down on Phelps' head with a force that split the scalp and started the blood spurting.

As Phelps slumped against the table, Buck tore the gun from his unresisting grasp.

"Not bad for a cow waddy," came a cheerful, drawling voice.

Buck spun on his heel to see the tall form of Davitt in the doorway.

CHAPTER SEVENTEEN

Mel Davitt stepped inside the cabin and glanced quickly about, his gaze fixing finally on the motionless figure of Phelps. He felt the man's pulse, raised his face, and lifted his upper lids to look at his eyes.

"Put some cold water on his head and wash that wound," he told Buck, indicating a pail of water on the floor by the stove and handing him a clean handkerchief he drew from a pocket. "I'll bandage him up. He'll be lucky if he comes out of this with no more than a headache."

He picked up the branding iron that Buck had dropped. Then he whistled softly as he looked at the brand end. "This is the Triangle brand!" he exclaimed, wrinkles showing on his brow.

Buck stared. He hadn't had an opportunity to note the brand in the fast action which had taken place. He had suspected that both Phelps and Trawler were connected with the rustling but what would a man who was rustling Triangle cattle want with a Triangle brand? He would be more likely to carry a running iron.

"Tell me what happened," Davitt said crisply as Buck began to lave Phelps' head with cold water. Davitt had taken a small, paperbound book from his inside coat pocket and was looking in it with an eager look in his eyes.

While Buck washed the wound in Phelps' head, he told Davitt briefly what had occurred, finishing with the swift departure of Trawler and the dropping of Phelps.

"I thought Screw-eye, or Phelps, was making believe he was crazy, but I dunno," he concluded, wagging his head. "I'd be willing to bet my chances in the next world that he intended to kill me, and he wasn't going to wait very long before doing it either."

Phelps' muscles began to jerk, and his lips twitched as Davitt bandaged his head. They then put the wounded man on the bunk. When Buck looked at Davitt again he was surprised to see him smiling.

"Trawler's liable to come romping back here," Buck reminded him.

"Oh, no, he isn't," Davitt said confidently. "He'll be gone all night on an errand and maybe we'll catch a glimpse of him in the morning. I saw him ride on up the trail, and I saw him light some matches to make sure nobody was riding ahead of him. I saw the flashes of your gun and came up roundabout. After I saw Trawler leave, the shots brought me to the cabin lickety-split. I'd already spotted the light from the window. Hope Trawler didn't think he could lose an old trailer like me by just turning around a big rock." He chuckled gaily and inspected the coffee pot on the stove.

"I'll have a cup of this while our crazy hermit is kicking out of it," he said. "I got a good view of Trawler's face when he lighted his matches. If I ever saw a born-to-order killer's eyes, he's got 'em." His own eyes sparkled with satisfaction, to Buck's astonishment, and then he pointed to the branding iron on the table. "Make anything out of that?" he asked, as he got a cup from the table for his coffee.

"Sure," replied Buck. "It's one of Lamby's irons. Maybe we'd find one of his checkbooks and his Sunday watch if we pried around this litter. If this isn't a crazy man's shack, I'll marry and settle down in it."

Davitt laughed. "Luck threw us together, Buck, and it has both hands tight around our necks," he said genially. "This crazy hermit of yours, now … take him. You found him fishing after dark. That sounds crazy enough, unless he really wanted to catch some fish. The big ones feed at night, they say. And he was using bait, you say. Doesn't that mean anything to you?"

"Means he wasn't sporting enough to use flies, or couldn't throw 'em properly," returned Buck scornfully. "I still think he was there keeping a lookout."

"That isn't impossible. But he was fishing, just the same. What was he using for bait?" Davitt put the question sharply.

Buck sat down gingerly on the edge of the bunk beside the injured hermit. "I suppose he was using worms," he said languidly, "but for all I know he might have been using chewing tobacco. I can dive into the river and get the hook." He started to roll a smoke.

"Quigley gave me more credit for being halfway smart than I thought he did," Davitt observed soberly. "He told me Lamby might have it in for Hull and suspect him because Hull was once in sheep. I've looked in the book and have found that Hull once had a cattle brand that was a star on the side. He sold it to an outfit up north. But more about that later. He was telling me something right along and I'm just beginning to get the gist of it. It's like putting one of those picture puzzles together. Listen, Buck."

He dropped into a chair, drank some of the coffee, and leaned forward, his eyes sparkling with excitement. "Remember what he told me last? He said people used worms for fishing, so why not use worms as clues. And worms are bait. Now do you begin to suspect what I'm starting to commence to hint about? Worms, clue, bait ... and Phelps."

"Meaning you're going to bait a hook with Phelps and catch the rustlers," snorted Buck. "Mel, old boy, guzzle some more of that chicory and take a deep breath. It works better thataway."

"I hope I don't have to write this down and draw a diagram," Davitt said in feigned disgust. "For some reason, and I begin to suspect what it was, Quigley, as Hull's foreman, didn't want to tell me in so many words what he suspicioned or knew. But he told me I wouldn't think that crack about worms being clues was a joke when I thought it over hard. Here we find this Phelps fishing as an excuse for keeping a watch on the Horseshoe trail. He's fishing with bait ... worms, you can bet. Quigley knew I'd scout around, for he as much as said so. He thought I might run across this half-wit on his fishing lookout. Then I'd remember what he said about people fishing with worms and my using worms for a clue. In other words, finding Phelps fishing and watching was a clue to the rustlers. He left it to me to guess it or figure it out. Listen, my buckaroo, Quigley is a clever man."

"Then you mean he meant for you to hook Phelps up with the rustlers if you were bright enough to figure out that remark?" Buck asked, his eyes brightening. "Then Quigley must know himself that Phelps is mixed up in it."

"Exactly," Davitt confirmed. "And something prevented him saying so. Since Trawler is traveling with Phelps, or using him, Quigley must know he's mixed up in it, too. But for some reason best known to himself, Quigley couldn't see his way clear to put me on the track."

Buck tapped his left palm with his right forefinger. "Quigley knew we'd go snooping around. He knew Phelps was a lookout, keeping an eye on this trail up here, and that he sat there fishing as a blind. So he gave you that tip. He expected we'd run across

Phelps and sneak up on him. I see it now. What's more, if this trail has to be watched, then it leads to where the rustlers are operating and probably to where the cattle are cached. Now that we know this much, maybe we can get Quigley to tell us more. Or maybe we can make Phelps talk."

"Those are both good possibilities," Davitt agreed. "I can almost see your brain expanding right in front of my eyes, bucko. Just to test it, I'm going to show you something else,"

He brought forth a pencil and drew two triangles on the back of an envelope he took from a pocket. "See those?" he asked.

Buck leaned over Davitt's shoulder, looked at the two figures. "What you going to do?" he asked. "Is it a trick?"

"Yes, I think it's a trick," said Davitt. "Suppose we twist one of those triangles a half turn and superimpose it on the other … here's what we get."

He drew the figure:

"Do you see what that would make, Buck?" he said with great satisfaction. "It would make a star radiating six points. Now if the cattle thieves who're stealing Triangle stock should be slapping on another triangle over the original brand, they've got a star, haven't they? And that star would mix pretty well with other cattle that had been marked with a star in the first place, wouldn't it? And Hull once had a star brand and sold it. So now what?"

"Whoever bought the star brand is stealing Lamby's stock and making the Triangle brand into a star and mixing the stolen beeves with his own herd," replied Buck promptly. "Do I go to the head of the class or do we have to find who owns that star brand?"

"Both!" sang Davitt. "Buck, this game isn't so hard once a fellow gets a start. It looks as if you'd tripped and stumbled headlong into the solution of the puzzle. The point, as I now see it, is whether or not the hombre who calls himself Trawler is the man who bought Hull's old Star brand. And maybe his nibs Quigley can tell us."

They looked at each other soberly.

"Fifteen two, and two ... are four!"

Both men started and looked at the figure on the bunk.

Phelps was moving his arms and legs restlessly. He was muttering, "Two for the pair, and one ... for the go." Phelps' eyes opened glassily and closed.

Davitt and Buck stepped quickly to the bunk.

"He's happy," Buck said, frowning. "He's playing cribbage."

"He's a sick man and he's going to be that way for a spell," Davitt said after he had tried to rouse Phelps in vain. "We've got to get him out of here and take him to the nearest place. I reckon that would be the Hull Ranch. Do you know the way?"

Buck's eyes lighted with keen comprehension. "It'll give us a good excuse for our visit to Quigley," he said. "Sure I know the way. It turns off from the Horseshoe trail to the left across the badlands. We might ..." He frowned and hesitated. "We might meet up with somebody," he finished.

"We've got to take that chance," Davitt said curtly. "I've a hunch that Trawler is on his way ahead of us. I can carry this fellow in front of me in the saddle and you can lead the way. My horse is out in the brush. I'll get him, and we'll start."

"I wish the moon would come up," said Buck. "I'd like to spot a cow with a star brand on it. They'd have to work those lines over a little in the brand where they cross, but I reckon it could be done. Something tells me that this thing works out too easy."

"That's where the trouble is liable to come in," Davitt snapped as he went out.

While Davitt was gone Buck examined the branding iron. There was every indication that it had been recently used. Perhaps this very cabin was used as the headquarters of the rustlers, although such could hardly be the case if there was a regular band. But since the thefts, as Buck understood, had extended over a long period, since early spring, in fact, it would be possible for three men, or four at most, to do the brand working. Buck searched the debris on the floor and found another iron, one which was broken. This seemed to cement the evidence that Phelps had helped with the branding and had been in charge of the irons.

When Davitt returned, Buck showed him the broken iron. Phelps was no better and Buck went out and got his horse. The animal had not even been unsaddled. Trawler had probably expected Phelps to take care of the horse. Buck became more and more impressed with what appeared to be extraordinary confidence on the part of Trawler. It might even prove to be a fact that he was working on the case after all.

But Buck respected Davitt's experience and the latter apparently didn't harbor any such idea.

* * * * *

A misty, cold dawn was in the east when Davitt, holding the now delirious Phelps in the saddle in front of him, and Buck rode up to a cow camp on the Hull range near a great herd of cattle.

To the surprise of both of them, and to Davitt's satisfaction particularly, it was Quigley, the Hull foreman, who rode out to meet them.

"Let me lead the talking," Davitt said sharply to Buck before Quigley drew up.

"By the looks of that bird's face, there'll be plenty of it," Buck shot back with a grimace.

"What's the matter? Is somebody hurt?" Quigley addressed his questions to Davitt after favoring Buck with a single sharp glance.

"This fellow was fishing last night and fell in," Davitt said, looking the foreman straight in the eye. "Fishing with worms for bait, so I took your tip and used 'em as clues, Quigley ... the worms and Phelps here, I mean. What you told me wasn't a joke after all."

Quigley was biting his upper lip, keeping his gaze locked with Davitt's. "Is he dead, or badly hurt, or what? Why did you bring him here?" He looked significantly at Buck.

"That's my partner, Buck Granger," Davitt said cheerfully, waving his free hand at the cowpuncher. "We're taking this fellow to the nearest habitation. That'll be Hull's ranch, I expect. Here, Buck, you take this squirming bundle a while, will you?"

The transfer of Phelps, who was muttering and talking in senseless jargon by turns in the throes of his delirium, was quickly made. Quigley signaled to a cowpuncher, evidently the night hawk who had been in charge of the horses, and the man galloped up to them.

"Ride in with this fellow," the foreman ordered. "He's got a sick man. Put him up in camp till I get there." He nodded to Buck.

When Buck had left with the other rider Quigley looked sharply at Davitt. "You might as well get off what's on your mind," he said.

"Sure," said Davitt amicably. "Just a question. Quigley, who did Hull sell his Star brand to? Think hard. I reckon you were with him at the time."

"Certainly I was with him at the time," Quigley answered crisply. "He had no use for the brand then. He sold what cattle were left and the brand with 'em. That was before he went into cattle strong."

"That's right," Davitt drawled. "He really had no use for it. And now he's got an original brand of his own, of course. Who did you say he sold the Star brand to, Quigley?"

"He sold it to Lamby," Quigley replied with a faint smile showing on his lips as Davitt straightened in the saddle.

CHAPTER EIGHTEEN

Mel Davitt looked coldly at Quigley until the smile faded from the foreman's lips and a frown came over his face.

"I suppose you're wondering about that," said Quigley. "When Hull sold the brand and the cattle that went with it, he thought he was through with cattle. I reckon that's why Lamby bought him out at his own price. Hull was in sheep pretty heavy and Lamby knew the sheep would have to go as the range got cut down. When Hull went back into cattle, Lamby didn't like it none."

"I suppose not," said Davitt. "Did Lamby use the brand?"

"He used it up to this year," returned Quigley. "Fact is, we've found Star cattle right on our range. He claimed it was mostly Star cattle had been stole. He hinted that he didn't want to go through our herds. That's when I ordered him off our range and Hull backed me up."

Davitt hadn't taken his eyes from Quigley's and he saw beyond the question of a doubt that the man was speaking the truth. He saw, too, that Quigley was incensed. On the face of it, to one less experienced, it would appear that Lamby was planting cattle on

Hull's range to enable him later to claim that they had been stolen by Hull or his men. Remembering the look in Lamby's eye when he had talked to him, Davitt felt convinced that the stockman was above such tactics.

It was Davitt's turn to frown, but he did so because he was puzzled. "You knew this crazy Phelps party was watching the Horseshoe trail," he accused, "why couldn't you tell me so in as many words?"

"Because I wasn't dead sure of any such thing," Quigley answered. "I'm not going to shoot off my mouth unless I know what I'm talking about. I don't even know how you got him and I'm not asking. But there's one thing I do know and I'm going to tell you what it is and then you can go to blazes."

The foreman's eyes flashed, and his face grew stern. "I could have gone out myself with a bunch of men and probably washed this thing up, but Hull wouldn't let me. He's only been in cattle big for three years and I guess he's too timid, although you needn't say I said so. But I'm here to tell you and to back it up any way you say that nobody on this ranch has stolen any of Lamby's cattle, nor bothered a head of stock with any of his half-dozen brands on 'em. There's stock of his mixed with ours right now and he'll keep right on his side of the range till the fall roundup, and then his reps can cut out his stock. And you're not going to do any inspecting of our herds, neither. Not so as I can notice it, you're not."

"You talk to me like a man that's trying to cover up a lot he knows with loud talk in another direction," Davitt said calmly.

"And you talk to me like a jackass who doesn't know where he's at!" Quigley retorted hotly, losing his temper. "Why, there's stock of Lamby's right down in the corner by the butte right now and how'd they get there? If you're so smart, answer that."

"From the way you're trying to cover up, it wouldn't surprise me a bit if you'd put 'em there," said Davitt coldly. "Don't make any false motions toward your gun, Quigley! I came here to talk to you, not to shoot you."

Quigley's face was puffed and red with anger. "I know your style," he managed to get out. "You stand behind your rep as a gunman. Well, you won't make any false showing by plugging me. I'll throw my gun away, call you a liar to your face, and then laugh at you, you sap. I've got twenty guns behind me to cut you down if you start anything." He put two fingers in his mouth and whistled shrilly.

In another moment the camp was in a turmoil as the punchers caught up their horses and rode toward the pair at a gallop.

Davitt held up a hand in a commanding gesture as the men rode up. "Have any of you men seen any of Lamby's cattle on this range?" he called out, his gaze sweeping the faces of the crew.

"I've already answered him about that!" cried Quigley.

Davitt saw the men nodding with puzzled expressions at their leader. "That's all right," he told them. "Quigley merely wanted to confirm it." He looked narrowly at the foreman. "I'm taking you at your word," he said sharply.

"And I'm ordering you off this range," sang out Quigley.

"That is something in which Hull won't back you up," said Davitt grimly. He waited a few moments while Quigley cooled. "Now, if you'll be so hospitable, Buck and me will have a bite of breakfast and be on our way. We'll leave the hermit party with you."

* * * * *

Buck and Davitt rode away from the camp with the morning sun streaming gold on the rugged crest of Horseshoe Butte. They rode southeastward, with the butte off at the left and the corner that

Quigley had spoken of down to their right. The direction they were taking would bring them to a point in the badlands midway between the butte and the corner.

Davitt was in a thoughtful mood. He had dumped the injured Phelps on Quigley and the foreman had ordered him taken to the house. There had been no further words between Quigley and Davitt, for the latter had been taciturn and had ignored the foreman completely.

When they were well out of sight of the camp, Davitt called a halt. "I was wrong when I had the notion that Trawler maybe had hurried to see Quigley," he said. "I don't think Quigley has anything to do with this rustling business. Something is holding him back, though. There's somebody higher up and I think it's Hull. I let Quigley get mad, *made* him mad, in fact, and I know he told me the truth."

"He seemed annoyed when I rode up with his men," said Buck. "There were some cows pretty close in to the camp down there and I thought I spied one with a star brand on it."

"Quigley said there were some star-branded cattle on his range," Davitt confirmed. "Said there was a bunch of Lamby's cattle in the corner down there right now." He pointed off to the lower right of the tumbled district.

"Looks to me like we better find out about the stock cache, if there is one, and let guessing take care of itself for a while," drawled Buck.

"And any man we meet is a rustler till he proves something to the contrary," nodded Davitt. "I've got a hunch, Buck, that we're going to smell powder smoke." There was no smile in his eyes as he said this.

They rode straight for the rugged strip of the badlands. When they reached the first of the tumbled ridges, washes, gullies, and deep ravines, they took the first trail that led into the heart of the strip that ran straight to the open end of Horseshoe Butte. This brought them to the dry bed of a stream where water ran only when the snows were melting in spring or after a hard rain.

Buck now was in the lead, reading sign in the trail and keeping their course true. He drew rein in the dry gravel of the long wash. "I've never been in there, but I've heard there is a big open space in the butte, rimmed by the walls of the rock horseshoe. It would be a good place to cache cattle and they could be driven up this creek bed."

Davitt was staring at a patch of sand in the middle of the wash. "There have been cattle in here," he said, pointing.

The tracks were easily discernible in the sand.

Buck hitched his gun. "We'll go up," he said shortly. "We'll have to walk our horses in this so's not to make any more noise than we can help."

As they proceeded up the dry bed of the stream they saw more and more sign that cattle had been moved there. In damp places the soil was tramped down by scores of hoofs, and at one of these spots Buck stopped and pointed downward.

"Shod tracks and fresh," he said. "Riders."

Davitt nodded and looked ahead. It was impossible to see any distance because of the brush, willows, and trees. There were great boulders, too, left there presumably by prehistoric avalanches or glaciers. The feeling that they were riding into a natural trap, which had been growing on him, suddenly became an absolute conviction.

"Make for that pile of rocks," he told Buck, pointing to a mass of boulders some little distance up the wash. "It's too open here." He started and raised himself in the saddle as a shadow moved on the chalky white of the gravel where the branches of some trees hung low far ahead.

He drove in his spurs and whipped out his gun as a sharp

report shattered the stillness. He thought a bullet fanned his cheek as his own gun blazed. Buck was to the left of him, his horse plunging in the loose gravel, his weapon spitting lead. The shadow took form as a man staggered across the wash and dropped full-length on his face.

Davitt and Buck were spurring their horses for the protection of the rocks. But guns were in action ahead and the bullets were singing in their ears. They could not see their assailants nor make out where the shots were coming from in that short interval of confusion when they were dodging overhanging branches, pitching in the saddle as their horses lunged and stumbled and rolled, protecting their eyes from whipping willows and brush. When they finally gained the shelter of the rocks, they found hard, firm footing for their horses and halted with the branches of a cottonwood interlaced above them.

Davitt was out of the saddle in a twinkling and he had hardly touched the ground when Buck, leaning from his saddle, fired twice. The gun was actually over Davitt's left shoulder when Buck fired.

A cry came from across the wash and then a sprawling figure toppled off a cliff, rolled and bumped down the sheer slope, and landed in a crumpled heap on the gleaming, white stones.

Silence closed in.

Buck slipped noiselessly from his horse. "There's another," he said in a guarded tone in Davitt's ear. "He's up around these rocks. He can get us easy if we start out."

Davitt pushed him back with his arm. He was looking up. "Keep out of sight," he whispered. "Come along if I whistle twice."

In another moment Davitt had grasped the branch of the tree and was climbing it. He gained a point where he was level with the top of the huge rock that reared itself up from the crumbled mass. Here was a great limb which reached over the rock's rounded dome. Davitt could not see beyond the rock because of the leafy branches. He lifted his hands, grasped the big limb, and, with the branch sagging with his weight, went hand over hand across the short intervening distance to the dome.

Here he crouched and looked down. He had made no noise, and none could be aware of his presence on the rock unless the disturbance in the branches had been noticed. He managed to slip down the rock a short distance to a niche where, with his feet planted solidly, he leaned back against the stone and saw clearly below.

In some trees to the right of the wash a horse was tethered. Then, behind a rock outcropping directly beneath him, Davitt saw a man. He recognized the man as Trawler almost immediately. He was peering over the rocks. Davitt searched the wash, trees, and the other spaces among the rocks but could see no sign of other horses. It flashed through his mind that the two men who had been shot down were probably lookouts. But he dismissed this when, looking intently up the dry bed of the stream, he caught sight of the familiar outlines of feeding cattle. On the right and left, the rock walls of Horseshoe Butte rose sheer above the trees.

While he had been surveying the scene, Davitt had kept an eye on Trawler. The man held his gun in his hand and kept peering over the parapet of rock. Davitt surmised that Trawler didn't know that his men were shot and was waiting for a signal or some kind of a move that would disclose the result of the shooting. From his position Trawler could see a short distance down the draw. If Buck were to appear around the mass of rock, Trawler could drop him at sight.

Some six feet down the rock from where Davitt was standing was a natural shelf which he estimated was three feet wide. Below this was a sheer drop to the ground of twenty feet. Davitt decided to slide down the face of the rock and take a chance on landing on the shelf upright. He had drawn his gun, but now he slipped it into his holster, edged along the narrow niche, and let go with his hands spread out on the stone coping.

As his feet struck the shelf he whistled shrilly twice, and his hand whipped out his gun as he went to his knees on the very edge of the shelf.

Trawler looked up—looked up into the black bore of Davitt's gun.

"Drop that six-shooter," came Davitt's stern command. He could hear Buck running up the wash. "There's only two of us, Trawler, but you can take a chance if you want to. Make up your mind quick!"

Trawler's gun clattered on the rocks at his feet. He kept looking at Davitt with a curious expression until Buck climbed over the rocks and covered him.

Davitt stood up. "Maybe you'll tell your old friend there what the shooting was about while I climb down," he said to Trawler.

He walked along the shelf to where he could scramble down the rocks. Trawler looked at Buck, who was scowling darkly.

"You figured the crazy hermit would bore me, eh, Trawler?" Buck said as Davitt hastened toward them. "Instead of that, I made him talk." It was a random shot, but both Buck and Davitt saw by the look in Trawler's eyes that it told.

"I reckon you didn't know that I took the shells out of that crazy fool's gun," said Trawler easily. He actually smiled.

"Why ..." Buck sputtered in his effort to get the words out quickly. "I've got Phelps' gun right here," he exploded. "You took mine and I took his when I knocked him out."

"Yeah?" Trawler jeered. "Then you filled it with shells from your belt." He turned to Davitt. "What happened to my men?" he demanded in a crisp, bold voice.

"They stepped into some hot lead," returned Davitt. "I'm not going to fool around with questions, Trawler, or whatever your name is. We'll take a look at those cattle up there and then we'll be going."

"I suppose you know that those are Lamby's cattle that I'm holdin' here till I can drive them down to the others I've recovered," said Trawler. "And those two men you fired on were helpin' me."

"Don't doubt it a bit," Davitt said cheerfully. "But it's the first time I ever heard rustled called recovered, thanks to you. Move along, Trawler."

Buck picked up the man's gun and thrust it into a side pocket of his coat. Trawler started for his horse and Davitt asked Buck to bring their own horses. Shortly afterward they looked over the fifty-odd head of cattle in the cache at the head of the draw. Each cow or steer bore the brand of a star on its side.

Trawler's eyes were narrowed and dark, but he held his tongue.

Buck had dismounted near a pile of ashes. He looked carefully at the ground. "Enough sign that branding's been done here to convince a blind man," he snorted, giving Trawler a look of contempt.

"We won't need it," Davitt said. "Trawler, ride along and we'll take a look at your friends and go on down for a look-see at the cattle in the lower corner of Hull's range."

Buck took up his reins in his left hand, held the stirrup in his right, and then shouted as he swung into the saddle. But Davitt was watching and saw Trawler's hand dart inside his shirt as he gave his horse a cruel dig with the spurs. The animal leaped in a frenzy of pain as Trawler's second gun roared. Davitt's gun answered three times with a staccato of reports that sounded like the reverberations of thunder in the bowl of the Horseshoe.

Trawler's right arm dangled, and curses streamed from his lips as both Davitt and Buck closed in and hazed his horse to a trembling stop.

"I've got a card from the Cattlemen's Association and I got those cattle back for Lamby!" cried Trawler, his bloated face purple with rage.

"Sure you've got a card," Davitt said calmly. "But it is a canceled card. I thought I'd seen your picture somewhere. But you forgot that Lamby's Star brand is a five-pointed star. By burning one triangle over another, and a little hair-working, you made a six-pointed star! That would pass all right on the Hull range and even Lamby might overlook it, but there's a six-star brand across the line and you could get rid of every head of stock you stole to the cutthroat outfit that own it."

"Yeah?" Trawler sneered, looking at his helpless right arm and the blood dripping from his fingers. "You say Phelps told you this?" He flashed a look at Buck. "I suppose you know Phelps is crazy."

"Phelps didn't say anything about it," Davitt said frankly. "But he got a pretty hard clout on the head, he's delirious, and it wouldn't surprise me but that he came out of it with a clear head, minus the cobwebs. That'll mean he'll talk plenty." He frowned and then spoke again. "Listen, Trawler … which isn't your name … you were a small-time agent with your first job with the association. You were fired for incompetence. I think you were more competent in another line than they thought. You heard that Lamby, Hull, and Quigley had gone to town. You sent Phelps in to spy around, and then made the mistake of coming in yourself and trying to scare Buck off in the bargain. You're just not smart enough to keep out of jail. You've rebranded about five hundred head, and we'll send word across the line to find out if you've sold any yet. Your worked brands won't stand 'put' for anything like till fall comes, you know. To be a first-class cow thief, you've got to think of all these things."

Trawler ground his teeth, but his black look of baffled rage only served to convince Davitt of his guilt.

"Now I'll tie up that arm of yours," Davitt said in a business-like tone, as he got off his horse. "Then you'll ride in peacefully or we'll tie you on your saddle … you can take your choice." His tone was not so affable as he said this.

CHAPTER NINETEEN

Buck Granger looked up from a letter he had written. He put down his pen on the table beneath the lamp and looked across the small room to where Davitt was lying on the bed, reading a book by the rays of another lamp on the bureau.

"How does this sound?" said Buck, clearing his throat.

"Sounds good so far, go ahead and read it," Davitt said, and yawned.

Buck read slowly, moving his right forefinger up and down as if counting time.

Mr. Sylvester Graham
State Bank of Milton
Milton, Montana
Sir,

Mel Davitt and the undersigned wish to see you at the bank at ten o'clock sharp tomorrow morning on important business. Kindly be there at the time stated without fail.

Yours truly,
B. Granger

"He ought to understand that, hadn't he?" Buck said in a satisfied tone.

"It's plain enough," Davitt agreed with a grin. "I wouldn't be surprised if he'd be there."

"The question is, will Lamby and Hull and Quigley be there?" Buck asked. "But Quigley promised they'd be there, when we saw him on the way down. Said he'd see to it. With Trawler in the cooler, and the cattle recovered, there's only a little left for us to do."

Davitt closed his book. "I think it's time for a night's sleep," he said, and yawned again. "I left word with the hotel clerk downstairs to call us in time for breakfast. Take your letter down and turn in."

* * * * *

At ten next morning, when Davitt and Buck arrived at the bank, Sylvester Graham not only was there but the door to his private office was wide open.

"Looks like you were expecting us," said Buck as he and Davitt walked in.

Graham looked earnestly at the two of them. "Tell me what happened," he said, but the crisp note he intended to put into his tone fell a bit flat.

Davitt explained while Buck settled comfortably into a chair and rolled a cigarette. "I took the liberty of inviting Lamby to be here this morning," Davitt concluded, "and I think that's him coming in now. Yes, and we asked Hull and his foreman, Quigley, to be here, too. We reckoned you'd want this thing settled amiably between all the parties."

Lamby entered with the same quizzical, half-doubting light in his pale blue eyes. "Good morning, Sil," he said in a weary tone.

"I got word from Hull to be here, but ..." He looked questioningly at Davitt. Buck emitted a thin curl of blue smoke and smiled.

"Here come Hull and Quigley," said Davitt. "Now we'll have a quorum. Sit down, Lamby. Did you go around and see our prisoner?"

"I did," growled the stockman. "I'd never seen him before."

Hull came in with his chest thrown out and a frown on his face. Behind him was Quigley, looking cheerful.

"Now you're satisfied, eh?" Hull said harshly, speaking to Lamby. "You're satisfied now, huh?"

"I may not be altogether satisfied," Lamby said, bridling.

"Now, gentlemen, just a minute," Davitt stated curtly. "Sit down, Hull, and you too, Quigley. Buck and I got you folks here, so everything could be cleared up to your satisfaction and this range made safe for the State Bank of Milton." He winked at Graham, who bristled and put on his best professional frown.

"It's like this, Lamby," Davitt began, talking slowly and earnestly. "You were losing cattle. All the cattle you were losing wore the star brand you thought. Were you sure?"

"The few strays we picked up wore the star brand," replied Lamby.

"That's it," Davitt said. "So you assumed *all* the cattle you lost were branded with the star. You hadn't checked up on it? No? I thought so. And the strays you caught, or saw, were on Hull's range, were they not?"

"Sure they were!" exclaimed Hull. "And he thought I was stealing my old branded cattle back, or some of them. Probably thought I'd claim I hadn't sold all the star cattle to him when I sold him the brand."

"That's just what I thought," Lamby confessed in a droll voice.

Everyone present with the exception of Davitt stared at him.

Davitt laughed. "As a matter of fact, you wouldn't accuse him of it, and you wouldn't try to comb his range, and you wouldn't report it to the Association because you didn't want any trouble? Is that so?"

"I was laying low to avoid trouble, yes, but ..."

"And you, Hull?" Davitt interrupted, shaking a finger at Lamby. "You wouldn't let Quigley go ahead and clean up the business because you thought Lamby himself was planting his Star brand cattle on your range. Now isn't that so?"

"Doggoned if it don't just about hit the nail on the head," boomed Hull, chuckling. "And while we both were laying low ..."

"Trawler, as he called himself, was stealing Lamby's Triangle brand cattle, slapping another triangle brand over the first one to make it a star, and actually caching the stolen cattle on your range till he could get a chance to get 'em away and sell 'em across the line," Davitt stated. "He knew the situation and he was working with a free hand. One of the men with him in the Horseshoe ... the one who wasn't killed ... says he'll talk. Phelps has come out of it with a clear head you said this morning, Hull. When he hears what's happened, he'll talk." He rose with a smile. "Seems to me you folks ought to get along up there." He glanced at Buck. "I'm going over to see Virginia Graham," he announced. "In fact ... she's expecting me."

"There's one thing you don't know, Davitt," Lamby said in his slow drawl. "Hull, here, didn't dare let Quigley try to clear up the muddle because he'd ordered me off the Hull range, and my men had an idea Quigley was to blame for the whole business. Quigley would have stopped a bullet sure."

"There's a question," Quigley said wryly as Davitt left.

Hull rose. "I'm selling my sheep, Lamby, and going in for straight cattle, and breeded stock at that."

"Then maybe I can sell you a thoroughbred bull," Lamby said, smiling.

"That would depend on the price," Hull returned, squinting.

Sylvester Graham rose and leaned on the desk, his face wreathed in a smile that was genuine.

"It looks as if it would be a good year, gentlemen," he said. "I'm glad this thing is settled. I thought, in the first place …"

"Not quite so fast," Buck Granger interrupted, lifting his brows. "There's still a delicate but necessary subject to be taken up. I refer to the … *er* … money end."

Sylvester Graham slammed his desk in undignified exasperation while the others laughed heartily, and Buck began counting on his fingers.

CHAPTER TWENTY

It was as sweet a noonday as the north range country could boast in midsummer. Instead of a hot wind and a glassy, scorching sky, a cool breeze laved the land and the sun smiled in an arch of deepest blue. It was a freak spell of weather that might last a day or a week, but not one altogether unusual in that section of the semialtitudes.

Davitt and Buck were camped at a spring south of the river, some twenty miles from Milton, where they had been making their headquarters. They had left Milton that morning and now, after a lazy lunch, while their horses grazed contentedly, they were sitting at ease, smiling leisurely.

"Well, Buck, so far, your proposition looks good," said Davitt with a nod. "The weather is nice, and I suppose the idea is to ride around, pulling up at favorite spots, and taking it easy. The thing that mystifies me the most is what need we're going to have for the five hundred dollars apiece that you insisted we bring along."

The cowpuncher grinned. "It was pretty decent of you to take a chance on my proposition, Mel, especially when I didn't explain it. I just said we'd be gone a week, and maybe we'd come back with the money and maybe we wouldn't. I figured if I could get you out from town like this, you'd be more likely to listen to the rest of it."

"Your reasoning shows a brand of intelligence which is unusual in a common cow waddy," Davitt said with a lift of his brows. "Sometimes I almost think I was pretty wise in hooking up with you. Anyway, it's been more fun than traveling the danger trail alone."

"Well, it's been sort of an education and considerable fun trailing along with you, Mel," Buck confessed with the winning smile that made him so likable. "You see, we've pulled off two pretty hot jobs together. Putting the Crow out of business was no cinch, and busting up that rustling outfit on the Lamby-Hull range wasn't such an easy order. I couldn't see where it would get us anything to hang around Milton, and it seems to me that we've earned a rest."

"Sure," Davitt agreed, nodding again. He made a lazy gesture with his cigarette, but he was eyeing Buck keenly. "We've both lived in the saddle most of our lives, so riding around this way will be a novelty, and there's no rest a man can get like lying on the hard ground with a prairie cactus for a pillow."

"Now don't get sarcastic," Buck flared, "and I never started anywhere yet without a destination. There's a town up in the Snowies that's so tough they eat glue on their hot cakes, instead of syrup. Doesn't that sound like a good place for folks like you and me to rest up in? And we're not going to do any work. We're not trailing down any outlaws, nor taming any hard birds, nor getting into any ruckus. We'll just stop, look, and listen, play around with our money just a little, and ... rest."

"I see," Davitt said wryly, "and eat glue on our hot cakes."

"Personally, I don't eat hot cakes in summer," Buck observed, as solemn as an owl.

Davitt stood up suddenly and looked about with an anxious expression.

"What's the matter?" Buck asked quickly, getting to his feet.

"Nothing, so far as I can see," said Davitt, scowling. "I was just looking to see if we were following anybody, or if anybody was following us." He resumed his seat on the grass and eased his back against a tree.

"Shucks," snorted Buck, sitting down again. "You're just naturally suspicious, Mel. I don't mean to say anything small, that away, but this business of man tracking has warped your judgment. You look at every man you see twice and think over what he says three times, that's what."

"That's a rule more people could follow without any bad results," Davitt said, and smiled dryly. "But, you've got to admit, dragging off this way looks queer. And you're acting mighty suspicious. If we're on our way to take a rest, why pick such a tough place? Seems to me a sleepy little cow town would be better … where we could doze in the sun, without having to swallow any dust from the street, where we could take a glass or two of beer without lunch and play cards at a dollar a stack. A tough town and five hundred dollars in a week spells trouble, Buck. What's more, I don't believe you're playing square with me."

Buck's eyes flashed. "I haven't got that coming, Mel Davitt, and you know it," he cried. "Anyway, if you feel that way about it, I'm proposing we turn back right now."

Davitt waved a placating hand. "Now, don't get riled," he admonished. "I've spoken to you before about the dangers of getting mad. Tell me flat how you came to pick out this town. What's its name?"

"Denam!" Buck exploded. "I picked it out because I thought we could enjoy ourselves there for a week."

"Both of us?" Davitt inquired with interest.

"Why not? You told me once you could enjoy yourself anywhere if there were people around, and there's people in Denam, both good and bad."

"But we're not to have anything to do with the bad ones, according to what I thought you said," Davitt complained, "and sometimes the bad ones are more interesting than the good ones. You haven't heard of any fat rewards up in the Snowies … money rewards, I mean, have you?"

Buck was looking at his partner shrewdly. "You think I've got something up my sleeve?" he said at length.

"No, but I think there's a joker in the pack," Davitt returned. He stamped the end of his cigarette with his boot heel. "Look here, Buck, you know very well that I've got nothing against going on a week's vacation, as you call it. There was nothing to stop you from suggesting that we hit the pleasure trail for a spell and you could have talked it over with me back in town. You would have suggested this town of yours and I might have thought I knew of a better place. You weren't figuring on taking any chances, that's all. You don't want to go to Denam just because you've heard it was tough. You've got another reason. I can see it in your eyes, boy. You're not so good at concealing your feelings. But, if it's a job you've got in mind, then that's right in my department." He nodded rather grimly.

As Buck had listened, his face had flushed a bit through its tan and he turned his eyes away. Now he looked straight at Davitt in defiance. "Suppose it's a personal reason. That wouldn't stop you from enjoying yourself up there, would it?"

"Now we're getting down to business," Davitt said, smiling. "I had such an idea from the start. Buck, I'll bet you my saddle and gun against a sack of makings that there's a girl mixed up in this." The last words came out with a ring of triumph.

"Denam's just as good a place as any," Buck persisted.

Davitt laughed heartily. "For me," he chided, "but no other place is just as good for you, my buckaroo. Why, everything but her name's written right in your face, Buck."

"You win," said Buck, scowling. "You saw her in Milton the first time I met you, at the dance that night, remember?"

"That neat little black-haired slip? Why, she didn't look tough enough to live in this town you're headed for … not as I could see."

"That'll be enough," Buck said gruffly, his scowl deepening. "She isn't tough and she's working up there. After all, you don't have to go along. I thought it would be nice to have you and they've got some fancy joints there, that's all. But you've been around a lot and you'd probably be bored. Suppose you jog along back to town and forget it. I'll push on and make my visit and maybe we'll meet up again. We've had some fun and made some money that will come in mighty handy. I'm sure enough obliged to you for my share."

"You earned it," Davitt growled, "and after what you've just said, I wouldn't miss this trip on a bet. Don't make any rash promises to …" He paused and looked at Buck with fresh interest. "By thunder, I plumb near forgot that you've got enough dough in the bank to get married on!" he ejaculated.

Buck leaped to his feet, his face flushing a deep red. "I haven't got any such idea at present, mister. After all, this is my private affair and I should have said so in the first place."

Mel Davitt rose slowly. "Not anymore, it isn't, Buck. You wished me in on this and I go. I'll take my so-called vacation in my own way. Now, let's saddle up and get started. No!" He held up his right hand with the palm outward. "There's no use in you saying any more. We go and, if I'm not mistaken, we ought to get there by midnight. If there's one thing I'm not doing, it's camping out when there's no need for it."

They rode southward at a faster pace in the afternoon. Buck whistled and hummed brightly, and Davitt chuckled to himself now and then, although he managed to keep his face stern. To the end of his days, Buck might remain a typical, carefree cowboy, but Davitt was not one to forget that Buck on two occasions had ridden with him literally into the face of death. After all, it might be better if Buck married and settled down. For Davitt felt that he himself would always be in the saddle on the high trail of danger.

Fate must have pulled the strings in laughing glee, for here were two fine examples of delightful, reckless youth.

The one thing Davitt was careful not to tell his friend was that he had once visited the town of Denam, and that he knew of some characters far from good who occasionally frequented the place. And this was one poignant reason why Davitt would not permit Buck to make the trip alone.

CHAPTER TWENTY-ONE

They rode very fast as Buck wanted to make sure of the trail while it was still light. They were cutting across virgin prairie, literally riding against the sun that was dropping fast in its western descent. On his one previous visit to Denam, Davitt had ridden up from the south and he was not acquainted with the trails in the northern part of the Snowies. He was depending on Buck's knowledge of the country, and the cowpuncher, in turn, was taking a shortcut and depending upon information which the girl had given him.

At dusk they pulled up on a trail that led into the foothills.

"I reckon this is it," said Buck, looking about to get his bearings. "Yes, this is the trail all right, for I can see the rock pinnacles up there she told me about." He pointed up the slopes.

Davitt leaned on his saddle horn and stared blankly at his companion. "Do you mean to tell me you haven't been here before?" he demanded. "And from what you just said, you are following a trail some woman told you about. Now don't get excited, but I can't remember ever having had any luck following a lady's directions."

"Yeah?" said Buck scornfully. "It happens we've hit this trail right where she said it was. I've been in from the other side a couple of times and this is a shorter way, that's all."

"All right, go ahead," Davitt sang out, pointing up the trail. "I'll keep an eye out for a camping site in case we need it."

"I'll make sure of my bearings on top of the first ridge," Buck returned confidently. "They can't lose me in a few bumps on the prairie like these hills." He pushed ahead into the lead.

"No, but you can stumble in 'em," Davitt called to him as they proceeded on their way in the fading twilight.

Davitt leaned down to scan the trail and saw that it was not well traveled. He looked up at the mounting hills with a frown. The wind had freshened and there was a chill in the air. Although the range was not large, it was not at all impossible to get lost or off the trail in such wild country.

They wound over ridges and through ravines, climbing steadily, as night fell. Finally, Buck pulled up suddenly with a smothered exclamation. They were on a level piece of ground with trees looming in deep shadow ahead of them. As Davitt brought up beside Buck, he saw at once what had arrested his companion's attention. At this point the trail forked and there was a sign that pointed straight ahead between the forks.

Buck was leaning from his saddle staring at the sign, which was plain as day—at least as clear as the moon and stars could make it. It was an old piece of board, with a crude hand whittled, and bore the faded legend:

TEN OR SEVENTEEN MILES TO DENHAM

Buck stopped, muttering to himself, leaned back in the saddle, and looked sharply at Davitt. "There's a fork here and there's the sign," he said in a queer voice. It was plain by his manner and his look that this turn in events had not been expected.

"Sure," Davitt said coolly, his gaze roving about the shadowy spot. "The sign's plain enough. It's ten miles by one fork and seventeen miles by the other. Which fork did your lady friend say to take?"

"Shucks!" Buck exploded. "I don't remember that she said anything about this particular place … just said we couldn't miss it, once we hit the trail." His eyes clouded, and he scowled to conceal his embarrassment.

"That makes it easy," said Davitt in an amused voice. "We go ten miles one way or seventeen miles the other. What's an extra seven miles on a vacation trip?" His chuckle was about to bring a sharp retort from Buck when he spoke again: "Hallo! Here's company. Buck, don't draw your gun."

Three shadows were darting swiftly in the space between the trees, and the night air shook to the thunder of flying hoofs. One rider was ahead, another to the left, and the third to the right. The sheen of the moon and the cold light of the stars glinted on the cold, blue barrels of guns as the three night riders closed in.

"Reach," commanded the leader sternly. "Reach high and sudden or we'll blow you off your horses."

"That's a mighty poor way to dismount," Davitt said, slowly elevating his hands. "You gents came along just in time to help us make out this sign."

Buck swore under his breath, but he followed his friend's example and reached as directed. "Sure you haven't made a mistake, stranger?" he said in scornfully. He wondered that Davitt hadn't seen fit to swing into action when the raiders appeared in such a suspicious manner. After all, there were only three of them.

"We'll see about that after we've gone through you," said the burly man who had issued the commands. "Get around there, you two, and take their guns," he ordered his two companions.

"Wait a minute!" cried Davitt. "Is this a hold-up?

"Don't be a fool and fresh at the same time," said the leader harshly. With this he swung his horse close to Davitt's mount and struck at Davitt's head with the heavy barrel of his weapon.

But Davitt's move was just as swift. He dodged like a flash, and his hands darted downward as he brought his own horse crashing against the animal the outlaw rode. "On the ground, Buck!" he shouted in a ringing voice. The next instant the guns of the raiders were blazing, and the horses were rearing, but in the brief space both Davitt and Buck had thrown themselves from their saddles.

This swift action placed the bandits momentarily at a disadvantage. The horses were mixing, stirring up a cloud of dust, while Davitt and Buck slipped toward the shadows prepared to pour their fire into the outlaws. But this move proved futile as two more raiders burst from the trees and raced their horses toward the pair on the ground. More shots rang out, and then Davitt and Buck were surrounded and stood with their hands in the air, fairly caught.

It was the work of brief moments for the bandits to dismount and go through their victims. Davitt was hatless, and his gun was gone. The fact that he was disarmed doubtless saved him from more than a cursing from the outlaw leader who was angry, but also anxious to take himself and his men away from the scene. A minute later the raiders were thundering down the trail and their victims were running to catch their horses.

"That's what I call taking a chance!" Buck cried to Davitt when they had captured their mounts. "If I'd had my way, we'd have started shooting the minute they rode out."

"Without knowing who or what they were?" Davitt snapped. "I've told you before that I don't start shooting before I know what it's about." He had found his hat and his gun where he had thrown them when the second attack was suddenly made.

"Night riders don't come busting out like that on honest business," Buck snorted. "Five hundred dollars and a gun. That's me. I see you saved your gun. Well, let's get started after that bunch."

"I saved more than my gun," said Davitt grimly. "I had a spare bank roll in my hat. I thought you said there wasn't going to be any business this trip. I'll lend you a stake and we'll go on to Denam."

Buck couldn't see his friend's face plainly, but he caught what he believed to be sarcasm in Davitt's tone. "Go ahead," he said scornfully, "but I'm not going to let that bunch get away with five hundred dollars and a gun of mine. I'll trail 'em alone." He whirled his horse, but Davitt was ahead of him, blocking the downtrail.

"Use your head. Those were only small-timers and they'll catch themselves," cried Davitt sharply. "You started me out for Denam and that's where we're going. Haven't you got it through your head yet that that's a trick sign?"

"What's that got to do with it?" Buck demanded belligerently.

"Don't talk so loud," Davitt admonished. "Don't you suppose if that bunch knew anything about the game, they'd cover their getaway? If they're any good at all, we couldn't start down that trail without running into hot lead. The big point is I don't reckon they know who we are. Move over here and take another look at this sign."

Buck followed him the few paces and Davitt dismounted. "Here's the joker," said Davitt. He grasped the square post to which the sign was attached, and it came readily out of the ground. He flung the sign down. "I discovered that when I ran against it in the fracas," he explained. "That's a fake sign and has no more business there than a tin jack rabbit. It's just used for stunts like this … to stop riders on the trail, get 'em bewildered, and put 'em in a position open to quick attack. I don't believe they had those last two riders cached in the timber at all. I believe they were just late arriving, that's all. A lookout spotted us a long way off from those rocks you pointed out. If this isn't a tinhorn job, I never saw one in all my life."

It was plain that Davitt was mad, and Buck was impressed. He looked down again at the fork in the trail. If the sign wasn't supposed to be there, it explained why the girl hadn't mentioned it. Now that Buck looked harder, he saw that the right fork of the trail was very dim and apparently had not been used for some time. There had been little travel over the left fork, for that matter, but it was worn quite a bit and was to all appearances the main trail.

"Doggone, Mel, if we'd looked a little harder … which we didn't really have time to do … we'd have seen that this left fork is the main trail." Buck pointed downward.

"I gathered that from the way those fellows rode at us," Davitt said, nodding. "We'll find their tracks along a way toward Denam, and you can lay to it there's where they came from. I figure that's the place to spot 'em. Now, let's get started." He swung back into the saddle and in a few minutes they were riding along a fairly good trail through the scrub timber.

At the end of the timber, where the trail climbed a bare ridge, Davitt, who now was leading, pulled up and pointed down at the path they were following. Clearly outlined in the cold rays of the moon and stars were the fresh imprints of horses' hoofs in the dirt of the trail.

"Keep your eye out," Buck advised gruffly. "If two of 'em were late, like you think, we may meet the rest of the bunch farther along the trail."

"In which case I'll have to do the shooting and you'll have to turn back," said Davitt, chuckling. "I still got a gun, anyway."

They rode on, however, without meeting any more riders. It was half an hour past midnight when they spotted the scattered lights of Denam from the crest of a ragged ridge. Another half hour saw them in the town.

CHAPTER TWENTY-TWO

Denam looked as ancient as the drab walls of the gulch surrounding it. Even in the waning moonlight, and by the yellow beams which streamed from windows on its short main street, evidences of several eras in its history were readily discernible. It had its inception in a cluster of prospectors' cabins, had blossomed in the boom silver days, had lapsed into a supply point for those isolated hills, and now lived, as the saying goes, chiefly by its wits. It was known as a resort town and a sequestered rendezvous for denizens of the surrounding prairie country bent on making holiday, and as a meeting place for those mysterious and often dangerous characters that ride the long, shadowy trails just beyond the law. The authorities had long since left it to its own devices.

Davitt called a halt where the trail entered the lower end of the main street. "Listen, Buck," he said in a voice that barely carried to the cowboy's ears, "I've got a hunch we better split up till we get the lay of the land in here. You ride on in, and I'll follow, casual-like, and we'll meet up later in the day."

"And I've got a hunch that you've got something up your sleeve," Buck told him. "If you're figuring on some kind of play because of what's happened tonight, you might as well tell me about it now, because I'm going to be in on it sooner or later anyway. I've got a half interest in that deal, you know."

"You've got more than a half interest," drawled Davitt. "You've got me beat by one gun. No, I haven't got any scheme in mind, and nothing up my sleeve that you could put a finger on ... but you're here to visit somebody and the right kind of people might not know me while some of the other kind might." He had taken off his hat and now he brought forth something and reached his hand toward Buck. The latter leaned from his saddle, a curious look on his face, and the next moment felt the smooth texture of folded bills in his palm. Before he could withdraw his hand, Davitt had left the banknotes there.

"This is a fifty-fifty party," Davitt said, laughing, "except so far as the girl is concerned. You might favor me with her name just the same," he added in a whimsical tone.

"Polly Peters," growled Buck. "She works at the State Bank. I really didn't need this money, Mel, because I can draw a check."

"Checks are always suspicious," Davitt snapped. "Besides, you might have to explain how you came to be short this way. I wouldn't say anything about the hold-up, if I were you ... not just yet, anyway. I wish you'd go ahead and let me have my party in my own way," he added shortly.

There was a sharp finality to Davitt's words which he had not used in speaking to Buck before. Buck was quick to sense this, and his mind was instantly alert. Davitt did have something up his sleeve. It was just possible that the man hunter, with whom Buck had worked before and who he had come to regard as a highly prized friend, might feel an unwarranted sense of responsibility for the successful hold-up. He might even have a plan to round up the perpetrators of the deed himself, in which event it would do Buck no good to argue. His best method would be to keep still and watch Davitt. He might actually put one over on this investigator with the formidable reputation.

"All right, Mel," he agreed, "we'll split and meet up during the day. No trouble for us to find each other in a town this size. I'm asking you for your word that you're not figuring on riding out with me missing. If it's going to be fifty-fifty, I'm entitled to that promise."

Davitt considered this, frowning deeply. "It's agreed," he said finally. "But I'm warning you, Buck, that I've got nothing in mind. Something might happen over which I'd have no control. But don't think I'm trying to be mean. Things were happening to me long before I met you. I just think it would be best for us to be separated at the start. That's all. And I wouldn't want any previous experience of mine to bust up our good time."

Buck suspected, from Davitt's earnest speech, that he feared meeting some former enemy, or the like, and wished to prevent him from becoming involved in any trouble which might ensue. This was white of Davitt and just in his style. Buck could not help admiring him for such a precaution, and, after all, now that he thought of it, he knew practically nothing of Davitt's previous life.

"You win," said Buck cheerfully. "I'm going to a house I know, where I've stayed before. You better take the hotel, and if you want me quick, just send word to the livery. I'll ride on in, like you say, but if you get into any trouble and don't let me in on it, I'll never forgive you."

With this Buck was off and Davitt noted that the cowpuncher did not ride up the main street. Davitt sat his horse for some little time in the cool mist of the night. His keen gaze roved over the shabby little town and his ears were attuned to the slightest whispers of that unearthly hour. Finally, he walked his horse down into the dust of the street and had no trouble in finding the livery. He put up his horse and carried his slicker pack to the hotel nearby, where he roused the sleepy clerk and engaged a room. Locked within the four walls of his quarters, he drew the window shade, rolled a cigarette, and lay down upon the bed for a final smoke before going to sleep.

Davitt's desire to be alone and the move he had in mind could never have been suspected by Buck Granger. For Davitt was seriously considering a duty which, he thought, it was up to him to perform—that of making a speedy exit from the cowpuncher's life and leaving Buck to think whatever he wished. Davitt had cared nothing for the danger involved in his own strenuous career, but to bring that danger into the life of another man, who he had come to like, constituted a perplexing problem. He fell asleep finally while the light still burned on the table near the head of his bed.

* * * * *

Buck Granger slept until nearly noon and then lost no time in meeting Polly Peters. It was a surprise visit, and he was waiting for her when she reached the house where she boarded, for her dinner. She was unmistakably glad to see him, but her greeting was shaded by a glimmer of doubt in her eyes.

"I told you I'd run up here one of these days," said Buck with gusto as they stood in the little front parlor of the boarding house. "Are you glad to see me?"

"Why ... yes," Polly said hesitatingly. "Do you give all your girls surprises like this?" Then she flushed.

"Come, now," Buck begged, taking her hands, "I haven't got any girl I like better than you, and I don't believe I ever had one I liked quite so well. Of course, I'm only a cowpuncher."

"But you're not a cowpuncher now," she interrupted. "You're in quite a different business, I hear. You see news spreads. It even gets up into these hills in a surprisingly short time. I've heard you quit range work and are ... are doing different ... work."

Buck saw the troubled look in her eyes and led her to the sofa where they sat down. "Listen, Polly," he said to her earnestly, "you mustn't believe everything about anything you hear. I just stepped out and made a little easy money in a different game, that's all. I'd never get ahead punching cattle all my life. It was all straight."

"Oh, I didn't mean that," she said quickly. "Of course, it was straight, and very dangerous work, too. You've got quite a reputation. It's just ... well, what I mean is that this might be a bad time for you to be here in Denam, that's all."

He drew back with an offended look. "You mean you don't like the idea of me being around because I've been doing some different work," he accused. "Some of the other gents hereabouts might object. Is that it? Well, I'm no common thief chaser, if that's it."

"No one said you were. If you're like some other fellows I know who are always jumping at quick conclusions," Polly said coolly, "you're going to get tripped often. That's all I've got to say on the score about this different business you're in. When I mentioned it might be a bad time for you to be here, I was talking for your own good. You've earned a tough reputation among a certain class, whether you know it or not."

"I reckon I know the class you mean," said Buck, scowling. "I call 'em tinhorns myself and I never had anything to do with 'em in my life. We're just on a little vacation, you might say, and I thought it would be nice to run over and see you. But if this is the way you feel about it, I'll beat it." He rose.

Polly Peters immediately grasped his hand. "Sit down, Buck Granger," she commanded. "Tell me, did you bring Davitt along?"

"Sure," replied Buck, sitting down with a surprised look at her. "Why wouldn't I bring him along? We're not on a job or anything like that, and he's as white a fellow as they come. I only hope he lets me stick to him."

"You're mistaking my meaning again," Polly said soberly. "I haven't anything against Mister Davitt, but right at the time it may be dangerous for you to be here with him. That's what I'm thinking of ... of you."

"Why is it dangerous?" he asked directly, eyeing her keenly.

"Because there's a bad man here, Buck. He might ... but you mustn't tell anybody I spoke to you about this. Will you promise me that? After all, it's just pure guesswork on my part."

"Of course, I won't tell," Buck promised stoutly. "If anything was wrong, I'd be likely to find out quick enough, anyway. Who's this bad party and why should Davitt and me be afraid of him?"

"I don't say you should be afraid of him," returned Polly. "But he's here and he's an outlaw. I don't know just how bad he is, for that matter, but I do know that the people at the bank are worried because he's in town. I was just thinking that he might resent the business you and Mister Davitt are in and might try to make trouble for you. His name is Bill Mady."

Buck wrinkled his brow. The name meant nothing to him, but it might mean a lot to Davitt. Then Buck started. It might have been this Bill Mady who had held them up the night before.

"Has he got a gang with him?" he asked quickly.

"I don't know anything about him except that he's in town, that he's a hard man, and that his name is Mady," replied Polly. "I haven't even seen him and wouldn't know him at sight. You'll be careful anyway, won't you? He'll surely find out you're here and maybe he'll think you're after him or something. They say he's a dead shot." She looked at Buck anxiously.

Buck laughed. "You bet we'll watch out. And we're not exactly afraid of these dead-shot boys, either. He isn't going to spoil our vacation. And we didn't come here looking for him, either." His face clouded a moment. It was probably Mady who had robbed them. "Now you haven't got anything to worry about, little one," he resumed with a boyish smile. "But it sure was good of you to warn me. Now will you promise to spend the evening with me, Polly?"

"I can't help myself," she replied, laughing, "since you came all the way here to see me."

CHAPTER TWENTY-THREE

Davitt woke, staring at the sunlight drowning the feeble rays of the lamp. He woke as suddenly as he had gone to sleep, after a dream in which guns were popping for what reason he couldn't remember. But the guns still were popping, only now they were the sharp staccato of knocks on his door. Buck, of course. Davitt looked at his watch, saw it was only ten o'clock, and frowned. He could have used more sleep.

"Wait a minute!" he called sharply, and the knocking ceased.

He rolled out of bed with irritation. Fine way to start a holiday. He walked to the door, turned the key, and threw it open, ready with a sharp remark fit for the occasion and his state of mind. But he said nothing as he looked into the black bore of a gun and then into the dark, mean eyes above it. For a brief space he didn't recognize his visitor, then he stepped back with a grin.

"Hello, Mady," he said, by way of greeting. "You here? Yes, it's you all right, but how come so early in the morning and why the artillery? Come in." He deliberately turned his back on the gunman and went to the table where he blew out the light in the lamp and took up his tobacco and papers.

Bill Mady stepped briskly into the room, shut the door, and locked it with his left hand, keeping Davitt covered with the gun in his right, despite the fact that Davitt had seated himself on the bed and was building himself a brown-paper cigarette.

Davitt gave him a quizzical look. "You don't have to keep that cannon of yours pointed at me if it tires you, Bill," he drawled. "You can see my gun hanging on the bedpost up here. I wouldn't have bothered to take it down even if I'd known it was you at the door. Funny you'd get the information so quick as to where I was. Maybe the liveryman told you, or maybe you followed us into town?"

Mady's dark, pudgy face darkened with anger. "Still got the same line, eh?" he said, with a snarl. "Well, since you came here to see me, and here I am, what do you want?"

Davitt lighted his cigarette, holding the match in a steady hand. The gaze he turned on the outlaw was cold and calculating. "I didn't come here to see you, Bill," he said slowly. "I don't know as I care about seeing you now, although I don't mind a talk with you. It all depends on where you were last night."

"Cut the ride around and come into camp with what's in your mind," said Mady. "You're not here for no table play, for the games don't run high enough. I happen to know you ain't changed your business none, and I reckon I'd be the only man you'd want to see here. Don't try no tricks, for I'm going to keep this drop on you if I have to make it permanent. That goes for all six slugs in this gun."

Davitt exhaled a little series of smoke rings and, though his eyes narrowed a bit, his general expression of faint interest did not change. "Why, you were never so bad, Bill," he drawled. "Fact is, you've got me guessing. You know I don't go out on small-time jobs and I've always thought that was your style of work. So far as I know, you haven't even got a notch in your gun, so I'm not very scared of you putting a slug into me, let alone six. I don't go out after anybody on my own hook even on a personal grudge. I get paid for my work and paid well ... and I don't take every job that's offered, either."

"A hired gunman," Mady said, sneering. "Maybe you'll tell me which side of the game is worse, yours or mine."

"Why, yours is, Bill," Davitt said calmly. "That goes without saying and doesn't have to be proved. If you were really tough, and pulling big jobs, I might have to set out after you sometime, but you're not in the class that attracts my trade." Davitt's smile was genuine as he resumed his cigarette.

Mady dropped into a chair directly across from Davitt and stared at him out of his cruel, small eyes. "Why did you want to know where I was last night?" he demanded, resting his gun on his knee.

Davitt had been thinking rapidly of a scheme that involved fighting fire with fire. It had been more than a year since he had seen Mady last and he had not suspected his presence in town. Yet it was just such an accidental meeting as this from which he had sought to protect Buck Granger. He studied the outlaw's face curiously and thought he detected a trace of blustering pride in the man's features. It was just possible ...

"Fact of the matter is, Bill, that a mean trick was played, out north of here, last night ... not saying that you played it, understand."

"Why not?" said Mady, with a sneer. "I get blamed for everything that happens around wherever I happen to be. If somebody pulled something last night, it must have been me, don't you think?"

As Mady put his question, Davitt caught a single flash in the man's eyes which caused him to smile to himself. "A man in your business, Bill, naturally gets blamed for a lot of things he doesn't do. No one knows this better than I. Is there any other cheap gang working out around here?" He put the question casually and flicked the ashes from his cigarette almost to the outlaw's feet.

Mady started and his gun whipped up, but the move was as slow as a branch bending in the wind compared with gun speed

Davitt had seen. Davitt noted this with another wry smile. "Don't get sore, Bill, I'm just asking a natural question."

"You mean a nasty question. I'm not traveling with any cheap gang, and I'm not working out of here, either. Suppose you tell me what you're getting at … about this dirty trick, I mean … and then we'll see." His eyes glared in resentment at a fancied insult.

"If you feel that way about it, Bill, I'm not going to come clean as a whistle with you," Davitt said in a voice devoid of any trace of friendliness. "I'm not putting this past you, for that matter. You're here, and I don't know of anybody else in your line that's here." He nodded with a grim smile. "That lets you in," he added.

Mady's eyes now were narrowed and cold, and he was possessed of a calmness which indicated shrewd calculation. "I'm waiting to hear about the trick," he said, his lips tightening into a straight line.

Davitt put his cigarette end in the ashtray with a slow, deliberate swing of his right hand. "There's a trail runs out of here to the north," he explained, "and there's a place up there about ten miles where there's a false fork of the trail near a clump of trees. We came through there last night and got hung up, studying a fake sign. This gave five riders a chance to bust in on the two of us and pull a hold-up." He leaned with his forearms on his knees and smiled at the floor. "In a way, I reckon, I let them get away with it. They didn't get much, and it was the tinhorn way they went about it which got my goat. We didn't even bother to chase them but rode on into town. A good hand at the game wouldn't have had to bother with a fake signpost."

He looked up suddenly to find Mady staring at him with an expression of incredulity. Then Mady leaned back in his chair and roared with laughter. At this time Davitt could have got to his gun had he so wished, but he merely glared at Mady through narrowed lids.

Noting this expression, the outlaw fairly rocked with glee. "So … you got … held up," he managed to get out. "The great Davitt … himself!" He went off into further gales of laughter while Davitt continued to glare. Gradually Mady's hilarity subsided. "Did you have that cow hound who's been traveling with you along?" he asked, wiping his eyes with his left hand.

"There's nothing funny about this, Bill," Davitt said grimly, "it was just dirt cheap, that's all. I've been spotted once or twice before, but it was done in grown-up fashion. You can leave my friend, Buck, out of it, because he took my orders. Another thing, Bill … this cowpuncher just worked with me on a couple of cases, and, so far as I'm concerned, he's through."

Mady grinned. "I see," he said. "He didn't come up to scratch, eh?" His grin widened. "I reckon the great Davitt is pretty sore." The smile vanished and Mady's eyes hardened. "And you think I done it?"

"Why wouldn't I?" Davitt flashed back. "It seemed to me like your style and you might not have recognized me since it was night time. I'm laying it right down flat on your doormat till you show me different."

"The old signpost trick," Mady said, jeering at him. "Well, if you want to know where I was last night, you go down to the Miners' Home, and ask 'em how many dollars' worth of checks I bought in a stud game, when I started playing, and when I quit. You wouldn't mind telling me how much they took off you, would you?"

"Don't worry, I'll look up your alibi," said Davitt. "They got just enough to make me mad, instead of making me admire their work."

Mady was fidgeting with his gun and looking at Davitt shrewdly and suspiciously by turn. Davitt believed he knew exactly what was passing through the man's mind. He was not sure by any means that Mady had turned the trick the night before; in fact, he doubted it. He was inclined to believe the outlaw's alibi would stand. And he could prove nothing if it didn't. But he was convinced that if Mady was not one of those implicated in the hold-up, he knew who had turned the trick. If this were true, it was reasonable to assume that Mady was considering putting himself into Davitt's good graces by giving him some information. This deduction proved accurate with a swiftness which was startling.

"My alibi will stand, all right, and I don't like to have you think I done this," growled Mady. He then put up his gun. "I'm taking your word for it that you're not looking for me for anything special. But what're you doing here, anyway?"

Davitt hesitated and then decided to clear away the last glimmer of suspicion. "I came over here with my friend for a week's vacation," he said in confidential tones. "He's got a girl here and I trailed along because I didn't have anything else to do. Now what you got to tell me, Bill? I can see something's coming and I hope it's good news."

"It was that cheap Dommey outfit," Mady blurted out. "They've worked that game a dozen times since spring, I hear. I might say something else if I was sure you could steer clear of peeping."

"You know I can do that," Davitt said crossly. "Let's have it."

Mady helped himself to Davitt's makings and rolled and lighted a cigarette. His eyes were brimming with the fire of his scheme. He leaned toward Davitt and lowered his voice. "Now we'll talk," he said.

It was nearly an hour before he left the room, and when he had gone, Davitt sat down and laughed softly. "The old signpost trick," he muttered. "And the old trick of setting a thief to catch a thief." He no longer had any desire for sleep and began his preparations to go out for the day—and possibly the night.

As he left the room at noon, Buck Granger was meeting Polly Peters.

CHAPTER TWENTY-FOUR

Davitt met Buck and Polly Peters on the street when they were walking back from the girl's boarding house where Buck had remained for dinner. Davitt tried to avoid them, but Buck called to him and in half a minute Davitt found himself being introduced to a brown-eyed slip of a girl who regarded him gravely and called him "Mister Davitt."

"Just call him Mel, Polly," Buck said gaily. "I told you he was a regular fellow."

"I wouldn't feel like taking that liberty with so important a person on such short notice," Polly said soberly.

"That's right," said Davitt, nodding his head, "if what you say is so. Who's been telling you that I am an important person?" he asked her, frowning slightly.

"Not me," said Buck, with a laugh.

"We hear things even up here in the hills," said Polly. "It must be wonderful … the work you do, I mean, Mister Davitt."

Davitt stared at Buck, and then frowned. "I guess you have been telling things, my buckaroo," he said severely. "I prefer to establish my reputation with good-looking young ladies myself."

Buck chuckled and shot a glance at Polly.

"Instead of talking, I've been doing some tall listening. I reckon I've got some information that will interest you. Polly, here, says …"

"Polly says she's going back to work this minute," the young woman interrupted, flushing slightly under Davitt's keen scrutiny. "Glad to have met you, Mister Davitt. I suppose we'll meet again." She left them with a queer smile for Davitt and a toss of her head for Buck.

Buck waved to her and then favored Davitt with a long look. "You can do it, Mister Davitt," he said sarcastically. "You can take the joy out of a situation and put a double meaning into it without half trying."

"There goes a smart girl," observed Davitt, as if to himself. "This is no place for us, out in the middle of the street … let's walk over to the hotel a minute." He took Buck's arm and they crossed the street.

"How much did you tell her?" he asked, when they were seated in the little lobby.

"I told her we were here, so you could look over your mining properties," Buck replied, "and then she did the talking." He simulated a yawn. "She had plenty to say," he added, in his delicious drawl.

"They always do," said Davitt dryly. "Glad to see you, I suppose. Well, she looks sensible, and she must have something in her head to be working in a bank, even if she does see anything in wandering cow waddies." There was a note almost malicious in his voice, but Buck merely grinned.

"Do you know a tough one named Bill Mady?" he asked casually.

Davitt looked at him sharply. "Does she know him?" he shot back.

Lowering his voice, Buck replied: "She knows of him. Says

he's a bad actor and in town this minute. Says maybe he might get riled because we're here, and to watch out for him. I told her we weren't afraid of anything smaller than an elephant, and she came back at me with the information that they're worried around town because he's here. I reckon this explains the play we ran into last night."

"Well, it doesn't," Davitt snapped, "but it may help us get a line on that play just the same. What else did she have to say about him?"

"Nothing much, except he's an outlaw and the bank's hiding its money till he beats it. You talk as if you know something about him, so tell me how his being here is going to help us get a line on last night's hold-up if he didn't do it."

"That'll come later," said Davitt, scowling. "I might as well tell you that I've met this Mady once or twice in the past, and again today. But I had no idea he was here, and he may bring us luck. We might even get back your five hundred dollars and your gun."

"You're not being sarcastic with me, big fellow," Buck said cheerfully, "not if I get the five hundred and the gun, and a crack at the tinhorns who pulled that trick into the bargain. So you know Mady, and saw him today? What'd he have to say?" Buck put the question in a tone that required an answer.

"Said he didn't pull the hold-up," Davitt said, frowning. "The rest will have to keep for the present. I suppose you're all dated up for tonight?"

"Oh, I can always break a date if the reason sounds good."

"Well, break it by midnight," Davitt ordered. "I'm going over to the Miners' Home later and start playing stud. If you can make it, be there ready to do the same at the table where you see me by midnight. This isn't just a question of gambling," he added mysteriously, to impress his listener. He rose abruptly.

"You have the fun and let me be the watchdog," he said significantly. "See you tonight."

He went quickly up the stairs, leaving Buck sitting in his chair with a nettled frown on his face. Then Buck strode out of the hotel and failed to return during the afternoon.

Within an hour, he was talking with a man to whom he had been introduced by Polly Peters. This man was tight-lipped, alert of eye, dressed in the garb of the hills. He listened to Buck with close attention and before the end of the afternoon he pointed Bill Mady out to the cowpuncher. But Mady didn't see them.

Buck kept his date with Polly when she left the bank, and none would have suspected that he had a thing on his mind except her.

* * * * *

As it neared midnight, Davitt, playing in a game in the Miners' Home, began to give less attention to his cards and directed roving glances about the room, most of which centered for a brief space on the front entrance. It lacked but five minutes of twelve when he finally glimpsed Buck Granger entering the place. He kept his eyes on his cards until he sensed Buck's presence near the table. At least the cowboy had had time to draw close. He looked up casually and caught Buck's eye. Davitt signaled to him and when Buck had unostentatiously circled the table to a place behind him, Davitt turned down his cards and rose from his chair.

"Take my seat for a spell," he told Buck in an undertone, "and remember there's more than five hundred dollars in those stacks of chips."

"Sure," Buck said genially, "and that's probably more than will be there when you get back. I'm not as good at this game as some others." He dropped into Davitt's chair and threw a swift glance over his shoulder to note the direction Davitt took. Buck had çaught a fleeting glimpse of Bill Mady huddled against the lower bar as he had entered the resort. Now, surreptitious glances, swift and sure, apprised him of the fact that no sooner had Davitt left by the front entrance than Mady moved toward the rear.

Buck had been rapidly counting the chips that Davitt had left and now he pushed the stacks of whites, reds, blues, and yellows across the table to the man in the slot to be cashed.

* * * * *

Davitt hurried across the street and up to the livery. It was the work of minutes to saddle his horse, which he did himself. Shortly after, he rode down the street to where the road started for the lowlands. As soon as he was out of the town and into the mouth of the gulch, dimly lighted by the night lights of moon and stars, he drew rein. It was perhaps ten minutes before he spied the familiar form of Bill Mady on a horse, riding toward him.

"I had to break a promise to my cow friend to take this trip with you," he told Mady in a cold, level voice. "Let's make it as short as we can."

"Won't take us more than an hour," growled Mady, "if your horse can run and we don't stay here talking. Come on!"

He spurred his mount and, with Davitt following and keeping a sharp look out along the sides of the road and behind, rode at a thundering pace down out of the mouth of the cañon into the sweep of the hills. They kept to the road for a distance which Davitt estimated as about four miles and then swerved to the left on a side trail that wound along the ridges and necessarily had to be negotiated at much slower speed.

Davitt's gun was in his hand, as he had warned Mady that he would shoot him down without hesitation at first sign of an ambush or any other trap. Mady had merely laughed and had said he could bring his friend along if he wished. But Davitt hadn't seen fit to do this since he had decided not to permit Buck to take the risk.

For Mady was taking him to the secluded cabin of the cheap road agent, Dommey, the alleged leader of the hold-up the night before. In the matter of identification there could be no question, for Davitt was certain he would be able to recognize the night raider at sight.

In a moderate space of time the trail swung down to a clearing in a clump of firs and they brought their horses to a halt.

"There you are," Mady said gruffly, pointing to a dim light in the window of a solitary cabin on the farther rim of the clearing.

"We'll leave the horses here," Davitt said crisply, "and go over and have a peek through the window to make sure of our man."

"Go ahead, I'll wait," grumbled Mady. "I've done my part in bringing you here and the rest is up to you. But remember, there's to be no killing."

Davitt felt doubly certain that he had been correct in detecting a note of subtle mockery in Mady's tone. "You better come along, Bill," he said suavely, "I might not be sure of my man." He slipped from his saddle and stood in the shadow while Mady muttered and finally dismounted.

They stole across the clearing to the cabin. Davitt's glances were darting everywhere, but he saw no horses or any movement to disturb the quiet of the night or arouse his suspicions. He kept an alert eye on his companion as they cautiously approached the window. The moment they reached it, Davitt saw it was curtained and that it would be impossible to see within.

The spark of suspicion instantly flared into flame. He whirled on Mady, his gun seeming literally to jump of its own accord into his hand. Even in that dim light he could see the startled look in Mady's eyes. Small likelihood that the outlaw had ever seen such a draw as that.

"Walk ahead of me to that door, Mady," Davitt commanded. "And keep your hand away from your gun."

Mady's eyes now were bulging and, as Davitt's crisp voice sounded the danger signal in his ear, his hands started upward involuntarily. Davitt made one step toward him and Mady turned and rounded the corner of the cabin.

"Knock on that door and go in ahead of me," Davitt ordered sternly.

Mady's knuckles rapped sharply on the door, the staccato of the knocks seeming to sound like pistol shots in the stillness of the clearing.

"Who's there?" came a voice from within.

"Tell him," Davitt directed.

"It's all right, Dom," called Mady. "A friend is here."

As the door opened, Davitt glimpsed the unmistakable features of the ringleader of the raiders of the night before. He stooped, so that he was concealed behind Mady, and shoved his gun in the outlaw's back. Mady stumbled inside and Davitt leaped in after him, slamming the door shut and covering the two of them.

"Sit down by that table, gents."

Both Mady and Dommey stared at him for one brief moment, and then sat down by the table upon which a lamp burned. Davitt stood between the table and the door, close to the wall and away from the window. A swift glance about showed him there were no others present. Mady's eyes blazed at him wrathfully, but Dommey's gaze was cold and snaky.

"This isn't an attack or a hold-up, you cheap night rat," Davitt said through his teeth, the snapping light in his narrowed eyes locking with Dommey's gaze. "I'm just here to collect what you borrowed last night. And then Mady here will tell you who I am, and you can figure your luck."

Dommey shifted his gaze to Mady, his face darkening. There was a question in red fire in his eyes.

"Better do as he says," Mady shot out of the corner of his mouth. "This is the great Davitt, and you're lucky."

"Never saw him before in my life!" exclaimed Dommey in a loud voice, looking again at Davitt and sliding his left hand along the table.

Davitt's eye caught this sly movement instantly and just as Dommey's hand reached the handle of a small bell, partially concealed behind other objects on the table, he leaped against the table, knocking the bell from the man's grasp. But Dommey brought his hand against the lamp with terrific force, sending it crashing in a burst of flame and shattering of glass to the floor. Next instant the cabin was plunged into darkness.

Two red tongues streaked from Davitt's gun as he leaped back and dropped. Then came the smashing of chairs flung at him and the cabin rocked with the roar of guns. A moment of stillness ensued and brought the thunder of hoofs from the clearing and shouts and shots outside.

"Lay low, Davitt!" rang Dommey's voice. "I want the dirty double-crosser that's in this room."

There were two bursts of fire from across the cabin and a gurgling moan. Then a double sound as of a sack of grain being dumped on the floor. One of the two outlaws had shot the other.

Before Davitt could figure his next move, the door of the cabin burst open.

"March out of there with your paws up … you're covered!" sang out the voice of Buck Granger. "If you're there, Davitt, don't move. We're giving the others two seconds to start moving."

"It's all right. There's only one other here." It was Mady who spoke and now he walked out the door with his hands in the air.

Davitt struck a match, holding it far to his left. Its flickering flame showed the body of Dommey crumpled on the floor. "Come on in, Buck," Davitt called. "I reckon we've got a dead one here on our hands."

In another moment Buck and another were inside, matches were struck and another lamp on a shelf lighted.

Davitt and Buck stared at each other. Davitt didn't know the third man in the room, although it was the man Buck had talked with during the afternoon.

"I told you that you couldn't leave me out of it," Buck said in a tone of triumph.

"So it seems," returned Davitt coolly. "And maybe I couldn't have handled this by myself as I thought." He smiled wryly.

"You bet you couldn't!" cried Buck. "Not with five of 'em layin' here for you, and Mady ready to make the sixth. Who's that?"

"That was our hold-up man," Davitt said dryly. "I broke my promise and left town to come here with Mady and get our stuff back, Buck. Now maybe you'll do a little explaining on your own hook."

"Sure," said Buck, grinning. "This gent is one of ten men the bank sneaked into town, fearing Mady was going to try a raid. My lady friend introduced him to me. They've been watching every move Mady made, and he knew all about Mady's visit to you this morning, and he knew all about Mady's taking charge of Dommey's crew, too. The rest was easy. We just kept a watch on you. I cashed in the chips as soon as I saw you and Mady leave the Miners' Home. Then all we had to do was follow you and Mady out here. We've got the others of the gang corralled outside. I feel pretty sure of five hundred dollars and a gun, and there ought to be enough in the bunch to pay you off, too. There's just one thing we got to have an understanding about."

"And what's that?" Davitt asked, frowning

"That you and me stay put as partners. We work too well together to quit now," Buck said, smiling.

"I was thinking it would be better if you quit the game," Davitt said slowly. "Not that I don't like to have you along, but …"

He paused as Buck called to someone outside, and the next moment Polly Peters came in, her face glowing with excitement.

"Tell him what you think, Polly," Buck said, pointing directly at Davitt.

"I don't mind Buck playing a dangerous game if there's plenty of money in it and he has you with him," said the girl seriously. "It is far from being a disgrace to be in your … your profession, Mel."

"I guess that hooks me," said Davitt, his eyes brimming with admiration. "I told Buck you were a sensible girl, but I didn't think you had it in you to plan a thing like this out. No, don't tell me you didn't, for I swear that I won't believe you anyway."

"That's right," sang Buck. "In this case, it'll have to be Davitt, Granger, and Company. And I feel sure there's some money out for this bunch we've caught that'll be worth collecting. Let's get our bearings now and start back. You can tell me about your end of the scheme later, Mel, although I've guessed most of it."

"On the contrary, I'll tell it to the company," Davitt said, smiling and bowing to Polly. "With your permission, you cow hound," he added, favoring Buck with a prodigious wink.

ABOUT THE AUTHOR

Robert J. Horton was born in Coudersport, Pennsylvania, in 1889. As a very young man he traveled extensively in the American West, working for newspapers. For several years he was sports editor for the *Great Falls Tribune* in Great Falls, Montana. He began writing Western fiction for Munsey's *All-Story Weekly* magazine before becoming a regular contributor to Street & Smith's *Western Story Magazine*. By the mid-1920s Horton was one of three authors to whom Street & Smith paid five cents a word—the other two being Frederick Faust, perhaps better known as Max Brand, and Robert Ormond Case. Some of Horton's serials for Street & Smith's *Western Story Magazine* were subsequently brought out as books by Chelsea House, Street & Smith's book publishing company. Although all of Horton's stories appeared under his byline in the magazine, for their book editions Chelsea House published them either as by Robert J. Horton or by James Roberts. Sometimes, as was the case with *Rovin' Redden* (Chelsea House, 1925) by James Roberts, a book would consist of three short novels that were editorially joined to form a "novel" and seriously abridged in the process. Other times the stories were magazine serials, also abridged to appear in book form, such as *Unwelcome Settlers* (Chelsea House, 1925) by James Roberts or *The Prairie Shrine* (Chelsea House, 1924) by Robert J. Horton. It may be obvious that Chelsea House, doing a number of books a year by the same author, thought it a prudent marketing strategy to give the author more than one name. Horton's Western stories are concerned most of all with character, and it is the characters that drive the plots rather than the other way around. Attended by his personal physician, he died of bronchial pneumonia in his Manhattan hotel room in 1934 at the relatively early age of forty-four. Several of his novels, after Street & Smith abandoned Chelsea House, were published only in British editions, and Robert J. Horton was not to appear at all in paperback books until quite recently.